The Blind King

Tales from Nōl'Deron

Lana Axe

AxeLord Publications
ISBN-10: 0692289542
ISBN-13: 978-0692289549
Cover art by Michael Gauss

For Lisa

Chapter 1

Efren placed a hand on his younger brother's shoulder as they walked down the stone corridor of the castle. Gannon led the way, his boots echoing against the polished floor. Their father, the King of Ra'jhou, had an important announcement for Efren, and Gannon had taken it upon himself to fetch his brother personally. Forbidden from traveling the castle unaccompanied, Efren had not even been informed that his father wished to see him. It was a rarity, as the king had little need of his eldest son.

"Are you nervous?" Gannon asked.

"Not really," Efren replied. He had a suspicion why his father had summoned him. There could be only one reason. His life was about to change, and he was looking forward to it. His marriage would bring him the freedom he craved. Soon, he would be able to leave the castle and experience life without his father's many rules.

"I wonder if he's chosen someone for me as well," Gannon commented as they continued down the passage.

"I doubt it," Efren replied. "You are heir to the kingdom. Your marriage announcement will likely be accompanied by a lavish feast." He grinned at his younger brother, knowing how much he hated attending any type of celebration, especially if it involved dancing.

Blind since birth, Efren had never been considered heir to the kingdom. When his brother Gannon was born, he was immediately given the title. Efren, however, was not bitter. He loved his brother dearly, and he had no desire to rule. Over the years, Gannon had proved himself a strong and honorable man. Efren had every confidence in his brother's ability to lead the kingdom.

"To the right," Gannon said, steering his brother toward the throne room.

Though Efren had the castle mapped out in his mind, he was never allowed to travel the halls unaccompanied. King Nilan did not want to risk embarrassment should the prince become lost within the castle's walls. His mother, the queen, feared he might wander away, never to be seen again. They had little confidence in their eldest son's abilities, and they looked upon him with sorrow.

Studying gave Efren his escape from the mundane realities of life. He loved learning of the diverse cultures of Nōl'Deron, and he particularly enjoyed history. His tutors would read to him for hours while he sat and listened, his mind filled with wonder. Having no playmates except his brother and sister, he had plenty of time to imagine the sounds and smells of the far-off lands mentioned in his lessons. He dreamed of traveling to distant regions, unfettered from the demands of ruling a kingdom. It was a great relief to him to be spared the responsibility.

Gannon spent most of his days training with a sword, but he made every effort to spend time with Efren. He did not understand his parents' reasoning behind naming him heir, but there was nothing he could do about it. His father's word was law, and he had resigned himself to his fate. He had proved himself a leader among the soldiers he trained, choosing to focus his energy on military activities.

Politics bored him, and he much preferred action to sitting around a conference table.

The pair finally reached the throne room and paused outside the door. Gannon turned to face his brother. "I'm sure the king has chosen someone pretty for you," he said. He brushed at the dark blue tunic his brother wore to ensure it was in pristine condition. Then he tugged at the black doublet he wore, hoping to make himself presentable as well.

With a quiet laugh, Efren replied, "It matters not to me." To him, the acceptance of his future wife meant far more than her pretty face. As long as she was good-natured and had not been coerced into marrying a broken husband, he would, in time, grow to love her.

"It's a matter of prestige for him," Gannon replied. "She'll be shown off at court, and they wouldn't want to encourage gossip if she were any less beautiful than a princess."

They stepped inside the massive throne room, where the king and queen awaited them. Efren drew in a breath and swallowed it, attempting to push away his nerves. The gathered members of court fell silent as the young men took their place next to their sister, Aubriana. With the three siblings side by side, their differences were obvious. Efren was fair-haired with pale, crystal eyes. He stood a few inches taller than his brother, but he was thinner, with less muscle. Gannon had striking dark hair and eyes, and a muscular build. Aubriana was nearly as tall as Gannon, but her hair was golden and her eyes deep blue. She wore a bright yellow gown, resembling the image of her mother, the queen. The princess's beauty was unmistakable. She had no lack of suitors, and she worried who her father would choose as her husband.

No smile graced the king's face as he looked upon his children. To him, marriage was a matter of business, and today was no different from any other. "Efren, my son," the king said. "I have chosen for your bride the Lady Ryshel. She is daughter of the Duke of Sarril. With the exception of your sister, she is the most beautiful girl in the kingdom. You should be pleased."

Efren stood forward and knelt before his father. "I am pleased, Your Majesty. I thank you for your generosity." Rising back to his feet, he felt as if a weight had been lifted from his shoulders. He had wondered if he might be sent to away to a different kingdom, but it seemed his father had other ideas. It would have interested him to travel away from

Ra'jhou, the land he had always known. He doubted he would ever set foot in the lands he had read about.

"My daughter, Aubriana," King Nilan said.

The princess stepped forward and curtsied. Her heart was racing, and her face was pale. Time seemed to stand still as she awaited her father's words.

"You shall marry Prince Ivor of Na'zora."

Aubriana's mouth dropped open, but she could not protest. There had been strained relations between her own kingdom and Na'zora. Skirmishes often broke out along Ra'jhou's southern border, and the Na'zoran king was not usually open to negotiations. It would seem she was the price of peace between the two kingdoms, and the reality frightened her. How would she be treated there? Would they accept her as one of their own? Though she tried to hide it, she was visibly shaken.

"You shall someday be queen," the king added. His expression was one of pride. Though he hated the Na'zoran king, he would gladly give his daughter to his enemy. One day, his own bloodline would sit on the throne of both kingdoms.

Gannon softly patted his sister's arm. "All will be well," he said with sincerity.

10

She wished she could believe him. It pained her that she was being sent away, and she wondered if she would ever return to this kingdom in the mountains where she had spent her childhood. Silently, she hoped that her husband would be kind to her, and that he was not as war-like as his father. Bowing her head, she said, "Thank you, Your Majesty. I shall endeavor to be a good wife to him."

"Indeed you shall," King Nilan replied.

"I shall have some gowns prepared for you in the Na'zoran style," the queen remarked. "You'll need to fit in among your new people."

"There will be no betrothal for Gannon today. He is heir to the throne, and the decision is far more difficult where he is concerned." The king rose and exited, leaving his children to ponder their futures.

Queen Cala descended from her throne and took her daughter by the arm. Leading her away, she said, "I can see your fear, child, but it is unnecessary. The prince's heart will melt when he sees you. No man could resist loving one as beautiful as you." Her words were sincere, her smile warm and comforting.

"I hope you are right," Aubriana whispered.

Chapter 2

Ryshel stared at her reflection in the mirror as her maidservant cinched the bodice of her dress. She smiled slightly, admiring the emerald green fabric. Today she would meet her future husband. Having full knowledge of his blindness, she wondered what tasks he was able to perform alone. Little was known about Prince Efren, as he did not regularly attend court functions, and few people passed gossip about the rarely seen prince. Ryshel's father had never laid eyes on him during his numerous trips to court, and the king never spoke publicly of his children besides Gannon.

"You look lovely, my lady," the maid said, stepping back to admire the future princess.

With a sigh, Ryshel nodded. "I doubt my husband is interested in my looks." Silently, she hoped he would be interested in her mind. Few women studied literature, history, or politics, but those things had always appealed to her. Of course she could dance and behave like a proper lady, but once she had her own household, she hoped to take part in running it.

"We had better get you to your betrothed," the maid said. "We mustn't keep him waiting." Opening the door, she motioned Ryshel to come along.

Her soft slippers made no sound against the castle floor as she proceeded down the corridor. The sounds of the banquet filled the hallway as she moved closer to her destination. Voices were speaking over each other, and glasses were clinking. As the door opened, her eyes scanned the crowd, searching for Efren among the gathered nobles.

Dozens of tables had been laid out with a variety of decadent foods. She searched the tables until her eyes finally fell on King Nilan, his golden crown gleaming in the candlelight. At the king's table were two young men, one fair-haired, the other dark. Immediately, she knew which one was her future husband. Taking a deep breath, she let it out slowly and stepped inside the dining hall.

A hush fell over the crowd as she entered, and the assembled guests rose to their feet to greet their new princess. She had black hair, which was pulled back into one long braid reaching past her waist. Her stunning green eyes, set off by her green satin gown, caught the attention of the royal family. Gannon and Aubriana exchanged pleased glances.

Aubriana leaned forward to pat Efren's arm. "Your bride-to-be is here," she whispered.

He smiled and sat up tall in his seat, his heart pounding in his ears. Hoping she would like what she saw, he held his breath in anticipation.

Reaching the king's table, Ryshel curtsied politely before him.

"Lady Ryshel," the king said.

"Your Majesty," she replied.

"This is my son, Efren," the king said, his hand indicating the fair-haired man on his right.

Efren stood and bowed to the lady who would soon be his wife. Taking her hand, he pressed it to his lips. "My lady," he said. Her skin was soft and delicate to his touch, and the scent of fresh roses graced her presence.

"My lord," Ryshel replied, bowing her head slightly. Relieved to find that her husband-to-be was handsome, her heart fluttered momentarily. His gentle features spoke of kindness, and she hoped that meant he would be a caring husband.

"Please, be seated," the queen said. "Have something to eat."

Ryshel took her seat next to Efren, but she had no appetite for food. Her mind was overwhelmed with many thoughts. Would her husband be willing to hear what she thought on certain issues? How many children would he expect? Would she be able to give him any? Where would they live? There were far too many questions when it came to marriage. Though she had been prepared for this event all her life, she still felt apprehensive.

Aubriana smiled warmly at her future sister. "I am Aubriana," she said. "I hope you will find happiness with my brother." In her mind, she hoped her own husband would be much like Efren. He was loving and thoughtful, and she believed Ryshel quite fortunate to marry a man who was both gentle and above her station.

After a while, the king declared, "Let the young couple have a dance."

Efren rose, taking his betrothed by the hand. A single violin began to sing, soon being joined by other stringed instruments. Ryshel noticed a smirk on the king's face, and she wondered if this was some joke at Efren's expense. To her delight, Efren knew the steps to the dance and performed each movement flawlessly. For a moment, she felt embarrassed for doubting him. In front of her was a charming young prince, and soon her fears subsided. She felt a sense of warmth in his arms as they moved about the dance floor.

Efren's heart was still pounding, but he concentrated on moving his feet to the correct locations. Careful training had prepared him for this moment, and he had no desire to disappoint his bride. The soft touch of her hand and the nearness of her body calmed him, making him feel as if she were already a trusted friend. When their dance was complete, he bowed to his bride.

The king applauded the young couple. "Splendid," he declared. Though he had little use for his eldest son, he was pleased to have him educated in the ways of the court. It would not do to have him embarrass his father, and it would be impossible to keep him hidden at all times. Though he had considered locking him away at birth, his conscience would not allow it. The boy was, after all, his son. Luckily, the queen had borne him a second son who could fill the role as heir to the kingdom.

"Shall we dance again?" Ryshel asked.

"There is a private chamber to the left of the dining hall," Efren replied. "Perhaps we could speak a moment."

"Of course," she replied. She was curious to hear what he had to say. Slipping her arm into his, she accompanied him into the empty room, her heart fluttering. "Shall we sit?"

"Yes," he said, taking a seat upon one of the cushioned benches.

Ryshel took her place at his side, wondering what he might have to say. She had been told to expect little interaction from him and to give him plenty of space. He had been described to her as a person who prefers solitude, but his countenance had a warmth that suggested otherwise.

"I would know the truth," he said. "Are you being forced into this marriage? I have no desire to make you unhappy, and I know I am not an ideal husband." His honesty came naturally to him. Truly, he wished only to please this young woman who had offered him her hand in marriage. If she did not wish to be his wife, he would make sure she was released from her pledge.

His words took Ryshel by surprise. The marriage was arranged, of course, but it had never occurred to her that she should object. He was, after all, a prince of Ra'jhou. Though he would not be king, he was still due to inherit immense wealth upon his marriage. She was guaranteed a comfortable life, and there was little chance he could be cruel. Marrying Efren was everything she had dreamed of. The fact that he cared about her happiness only made him more appealing.

Looking into his crystal eyes, she felt a connection to this humble man. Without a doubt, he would make a fine husband. "It is my desire to be your wife."

He leaned in and kissed her cheek, lingering long enough to feel her warmth. "We shall have our own household, away from the court. It is my desire to live in the country." Lovingly he placed his hand against her cheek, his fingers finding her soft raven locks.

"That would please me as well," she replied. It would seem that all her childhood dreams were about to come true. She would have a loving husband and a house in the country where all her needs would be fulfilled.

Chapter 3

Four decorated carriages prepared to escort Princess Aubriana to her new home in Na'zora. Her nerves had not left her, but she had accepted the situation and held her head proudly as she descended the castle steps. Shala, her most trusted handmaiden, would accompany her, giving her some sense of her former life. Starting over with no familiar face to look upon would have been devastating.

Gannon, Efren, and Ryshel waited beside the carriages to wish farewell to the young princess. There was no sign of the king or queen. Aubriana slowly approached her brothers, making every effort to smile despite the absence of her parents. She may never have the chance to see them again. Any visit to Ra'jhou would have to be approved by her husband, and she had no way of knowing whether he would allow such a thing. The two kingdoms were hardly friends, and she knew nothing of the man she was to marry.

Gannon took both of her hands and said, "My dear sister, your marriage will ensure peace with our neighbor to the south. May your husband treat you well." He kissed her cheek before departing for his morning sparring session. He wasn't a fan of long goodbyes. Though he would miss his young sister dearly, he was accepting of her fate. Perhaps they would see each other again someday.

Aubriana's eyes filled with tears as she watched her brother walk away. She dabbed at the corners of her eyes with a handkerchief before feigning a smile for Efren and Ryshel. "May your marriage be a fruitful one," she said. "I regret I must leave before this afternoon's ceremony."

Efren wrapped his arms around her and said, "Be well, Sister. May all your days be happy ones."

Ryshel said, "I regret I did not arrive sooner. I would love to know you better."

Her words cheered Aubriana a little. "I shall write to you, if you like." She sniffled quietly, her eyes glistening from uncried tears.

"I would like that very much," Ryshel replied. She kissed Aubriana on both cheeks and hugged her tightly. Ryshel was fully aware of the pain involved in leaving one's family. It was the duty of many noblewomen to be sent away to husbands they did not know. Her marriage had taken her halfway across the kingdom, but her husband's plan of country living would place her closer to her own family. She considered herself among the luckiest women in Ra'jhou.

Aubriana turned to take one last look upon the castle where she had grown up. Backing up to the Wrathful Mountains, the castle appeared as a fairytale land to her eyes. Fond memories of playing with her brothers and learning how to dance filled her mind. She wished with all her heart she did not have to leave. Surely Na'zora's palace would be a thing of beauty, but her heart would ever lie here among the mountains.

Finally, she stepped inside the carriage, followed by her servant. As the door closed, she stared out of the window, hoping to catch a glimpse of her parents. They were not near the entrance, nor were they present on the balcony leading from their chambers. They had not spared a moment to say goodbye to their only daughter. Regretfully, she looked again upon

Ryshel and Efren as they stood arm in arm. They appeared genuinely happy, and she hoped only good things for them. For herself, she hoped her husband would be as kind as her brothers had always been to her.

Efren and Ryshel lifted their hands in farewell to the princess as the carriages began to roll away. Aubriana waved back, her tears spilling over. Would she ever see either of them again? Only time would tell.

"My lady, you should not weep," Shala said. Tucking in a loose strand of hair on the princess's head, she said, "You are too beautiful for tears. A smile suits you better."

Aubriana managed a weak smile. "Thank you, Shala. I'm all right." In truth, she was far from all right. Too much was uncertain, and the reality of leaving home had not set in until she was inside the carriage. She made up her mind to sleep as much as possible during the journey. The hours she was awake would no doubt be filled with worry, so sleep would help pass the time. Tucked in her bodice was a small pouch of herbs that would ensure a calm mind and dreamless sleep.

Ryshel waited for the carriage to move out of sight before escorting her betrothed back inside the castle. "I hope she will find happiness as I have," she said.

Efren kissed her cheek. "She will," he said with confidence. "Now, it's time we were dressed for our wedding."

"I suppose it is," she agreed. Their marriage would take place in a matter of hours, and the king would expect it to happen without delay. He was a man who hated to be kept waiting, and this was an occasion for celebration, not a king's anger.

A manservant in a dark red tunic approached them in the hallway. Bowing, he said, "I've come to escort Prince Efren to his chambers for dressing."

Efren turned and smiled at his bride-to-be. "I shall be with you again soon," he said, kissing her on the forehead.

"I leave him to your care," she said to the servant, who bowed a second time. Ryshel returned to her own room to find several servants buzzing about.

"There you are, my lady," one of them said. "We must get you ready."

Ryshel allowed herself to be undressed and sat patiently in her undergarments as two servants fussed over her hair. She preferred something simple, but the maidservants wouldn't hear of it. After nearly two hours, they had finished an intricate style that stood several inches off the top of her head. There were braids and loops and long tresses dangling on each side of her face. She had never seen any hairstyle so complicated.

A silver wedding gown was brought out for her to wear. It was a lovely dress with sparkling threads arranged throughout. All of the dresses she brought from home paled in comparison. Her life as a princess was about to begin, and she made a mental note to hire a tailor. If she was to attend court functions, she would need better clothes than the ones she owned. Her family had been far from poor, but a princess was expected to outshine everyone else in the room.

On the opposite side of the castle, Efren was dressed in a blue-and-gold satin tunic. A circlet of silver was placed upon his head. The servants complimented him on his looks, and he smiled politely in return. He felt slightly nervous at becoming a husband, as he had not had any prior experience with women. Gannon roamed freely about the castle and encountered many young maidens, but Efren was given little opportunity to be alone. There was not a moment he could remember when no one was at his side. The king had demanded that a servant sleep in the corner of his bedroom, should he require any assistance in the night. This left little opportunity to experiment with women.

After today, Efren would make his own rules. With a loving wife at his side, he would preside over his own household and have children of his own. He looked forward to being a father and hoped he would make a good one.

The servants accompanied him to the castle courtyard, where the king and queen were seated. Gannon had also cleaned up from his morning activities, and he stood at attention near his father, dressed in a dashing red doublet. A crowd of citizens had gathered to witness the ceremony, and the noise of hundreds of voices filled Efren's ears. He was led first before his parents, to whom he bowed before being taken to the altar.

As Ryshel appeared before the crowd, the citizens cheered to welcome this new member to the royal household. The shining threads of her gown caught the afternoon sunlight, giving her a radiant glow. She dipped her head shyly, being unaccustomed to receiving so much attention. Curtsying before her future in-laws, she proceeded to the altar next to Efren.

His heart raced at her approach, the rustle of her gown announcing her nearness. Extending his hand, he closed his eyes as her small fingers interlaced with his. Her grip was delicate yet strong, and he savored this moment.

Lifting a golden chalice from the altar, Ryshel declared, "I take you, Efren, as my husband. I shall love only you for the rest of my days." Taking a small sip of purple wine, she passed the goblet to her husband.

Grasping the goblet and holding it high, he said, "I take you, Ryshel, as my wife. I shall love none but you for the rest of my days." He took a long sip of the wine before placing the cup back on the altar. Taking his wife in his arms, he kissed her long and full upon her lips. Before releasing her, he nestled his face in her dark hair, inhaling its pleasing fragrance. The crowd erupted in cheers, many of them throwing flower petals as the couple made their way back to the castle.

The king and queen rose and applauded the young pair, before following them inside. The occasion had gone smoothly, and the king was pleased with himself.

The young couple would undoubtedly come to love each other.

"Once the marriage is consummated, you may leave for your own house," the king said to his son. "Everything has been prepared. You will have the funds you need, and you will no longer be a burden to me."

Efren said nothing as the king walked away. Ryshel felt anger rise in her, but she also remained silent, not daring to insult the king. His footsteps grew fainter as he walked away, leaving the young couple in peace.

"Don't worry about him," Efren said, sensing Ryshel's displeasure. "He has never come to terms with having a less-than-perfect child. I am happy to be leaving his care."

"You are your own master now," Ryshel replied.

Chapter 4

After spending several days cramped in a carriage, Aubriana's body ached. The wooden wheels were not forgiving when they encountered a bump, and the longer she sat in her seat, the more bruised she became. Finally, they reached Na'zora's palace district near the sea, where King Tyrol dwelt. Aubriana's first glimpse of the ocean took her breath away as she stared out the tiny window of her carriage.

"It's beautiful," she said.

Shala nodded, her eyes staring off into the blue.

Stepping out of the carriage, Aubriana took a moment to stretch her back. "I'll need a bath immediately," she said. "We must take care to avoid Prince Ivor at all costs. He mustn't see me before I'm prepared." Lightly touching her hair, she knew it was a mess. Her future husband would certainly be displeased if he saw her in her current state. She planned to shine when he first laid eyes on her.

Five servants appeared out of nowhere to assist with her luggage and escort her to her rooms. The princess smiled nervously, wondering what they must think of her. She was probably the first Ra'jhouan they had seen, and she looked dreadful after her travels.

"This way, my lady," a servant said. "Your rooms are in the east wing." The servant turned immediately and proceeded up the palace steps.

Aubriana hoped that being in the east wing meant her rooms would look to the ocean. It would be a welcome sight to see such beauty each morning. She followed the servant up two flights of stairs and across a polished marble hallway before arriving at her chambers. To her delight, the spacious rooms included a balcony, where she could stand and admire the sea beneath her. There were velvet drapes and cushioned chairs all around, providing a suitable area to entertain her ladies in waiting. A large fireplace graced the far wall, and gold candelabrums would provide light in the evening. A tub had already been prepared in anticipation of her needs, and the servants hurried away to fetch warm water.

Shala began unlacing the princess's dress, while Aubriana pulled out the pins that once held her hair in place. She ran her fingers through her disheveled locks in a feeble attempt to smooth them.

"I'll fix them, my lady," Shala said, moving Aubriana's hand away. "Don't worry."

Aubriana's heart was pounding, and she wondered if her maid could hear it. After a few moments, the servants returned with buckets of warm water. Aubriana climbed inside the tub and felt immediate relief.

"My rosewater," she said. "I can't remember which bag it's in."

"I know just where to find it," Shala replied calmly. "Relax."

Aubriana settled into the tub and closed her eyes. Focusing on her breathing, she tried to stop her mind from racing. If the prince was displeased with her in any way, she feared for her future. She must impress him with her beauty first and then let him get to know her. All her life she had been taught to conform to her husband's wishes. Now, it was time for her to perform her duties and become a perfect wife. What if she failed? The thought did nothing to ease her mind, and tears came to her eyes.

"Shala, what shall I do if he dislikes me?"

"Shhh," the maid replied as she added rosewater to the bath. "He will love you the moment he sees you. There could be no other as beautiful as my lady." She stroked Aubriana's hair softly with a shell comb.

"I wish that might be true," the princess replied. *But what if he doesn't?* The warm water comforted her, allowing her to drift off to sleep. As dreams of her wedding filled her mind, a disturbance at her chamber door forced her back to reality.

"My lady," Shala said. "A servant of the prince is insisting you make yourself presentable. The prince is awaiting you. Your wedding is to be immediate."

Aubriana sat up in her tub. "Now?" She had yet to meet her husband, and she was not expecting to be wed the moment she arrived. Rising to her feet, she said, "Help me, Shala."

Shala rushed to her side, wrapping her in a white robe. "We'll have you ready in no time," she promised.

Aubriana's heart was racing as she hurried to her mirror. "Bring my finest gown," she said. "It seems I won't have time to choose a wedding dress." As she stared at her features in the mirror, she found it impossible to smile. Behind her, a group of young girls had entered the room to prepare her for her wedding.

Shala tied the princess into a long, champagne-colored gown. Her fingers worked quickly at the lacings, and Aubriana took shallow breaths to allow herself to be cinched tightly into the bodice. The young girls began fussing over her hair, adding pearls and sparkling shells to her golden locks. Her lips were painted soft pink, and her cheeks were given a rosy hue.

"How do I look?" she asked nervously.

"You're the loveliest woman in the kingdom," Shala replied, beaming.

Aubriana said nothing as she followed her servants out of the room and down the long palace corridor. She felt as if she might faint but did her best to remain calm. Entering a small chamber adorned with velvet tapestries, she finally glimpsed her future husband. He stood tall and proud near the altar, his expression severe. He had sandy hair and dark eyes, as well as a nicely groomed beard. Aubriana found him rather plain for a prince, but she hoped his lack of beauty might be replaced by kindness.

Prince Ivor looked her over with contempt. Marrying the daughter of his enemy was his father's idea—one that he reluctantly agreed to. As she approached, he grabbed the goblet from the altar and thrust it at her without a word.

Aubriana was surprised by his gesture, but she reached out for the goblet, her face remaining calm. Due to their common ancestry, the two kingdoms performed the same marriage ritual, which meant Aubriana knew exactly what to do. "I take you, Prince Ivor for my husband. I shall love and honor you for the rest of my days," she said before sipping the wine. She handed the goblet back to the prince with a shy smile upon her lips.

Snatching the goblet from her hand, he said, "I take you for my bride." Rather than sip the wine, he threw the goblet to the ground with a loud *clang*.

The assembled nobles gasped and muttered among themselves. Aubriana was startled but remained composed. This was not the time to upset her husband.

"I have no desire for you," he declared. "But you are my wife now, and I shall do what I must, no matter how it disgusts me." With those words he stormed out of the room, leaving behind his new bride.

Shala, who had been watching from the back of the room, rushed to the princess in time to prevent her from collapsing. Aubriana wept, her face pressed against her maid's shoulder as the nobles made their way to the exit. No one spoke a word to the new Na'zoran princess.

"I fear I'm destined for unhappiness," she said.

"Hush," Shala said. "All will be well. You will see."

Her words did nothing to comfort Aubriana. Determined not to live a life of misery, Aubriana resolved to conform to her husband's desires. If he preferred a wife who would keep to herself and leave him to his own devices, she would gladly oblige.

Chapter 5

King Tyrol stood at his map table studying the boundaries of his realm. During the last few years, his figure had grown less muscular and more round, and the majority of his gray hair had left his head. Peace did not sit well with him. It had aged him and caused him to grow fat. He yearned for action to fill his days, as it had in his youth. Conflict with Ra'jhou had given him vigor in those years, and he lusted to feel so alive once more.

Prince Ivor strode into his father's study, a stern expression on his face. The king looked at his son with a smirk.

"How was your wedding night?" he asked.

"I did what was necessary," Ivor replied.

"She is beautiful," the king admitted. "I would think you would be pleased."

"I have no desire for that woman. She is my enemy."

"Be that as it may, the marriage was necessary," Tyrol replied. "If we are to give Na'zora a sense of security, we must play their little game of peace."

"I fail to see the point," Ivor said. "It would be better to invade without involving a silly girl."

"That, my son, is where you fail to understand the need for subtlety. Open war would only lead Nilan to prepare an army of his own. Look at them now. Their defenses are weak, their army is ill-equipped, and they have no allies to assist them. They truly believe we are dedicated to keeping the peace."

"Congratulations, Father," Ivor said with sarcasm.

"They have no idea of my true plans," the king said, anger rising in his voice. "You would do well to learn a thing or two about your enemy. Why make an invasion harder than necessary? We want to expand our borders, not sacrifice soldiers. With our allies on the islands and our enemy complacent, we are assured a swift victory with minimal cost."

Ivor laughed. "Minimal? Those elves are robbing you blind. You're too consumed with your plans to see it."

Tyrol slammed his fist against the table. "Those expenses are necessary! No one in Nōl'Deron could train our mages the way the elves can. Without their training and potions, we would have no fire mages. That would be unacceptable!"

Ivor shook his head. "Our people have won victory for generations without the need of elves or magic. You are taking the easy road."

"Why shouldn't I?" the king asked. "This path leads to certain victory and a place of honor in the annals of history."

"We come to the truth at last," Ivor said with a grin. "My father wishes to be remembered as a great war leader."

"Naturally," the king admitted. "I will lead my army to victory, and you shall be at my side."

"But when can we strike?" Ivor asked, fire blazing in his eyes. All his life he had trained for battle, but peace with Ra'jhou had prevented him from riding against them. Yes, there had been petty skirmishes along the border, but outright war had escaped him. Now, he would experience the thrill of riding into battle and facing his enemy on a larger scale. His dream of fighting open war in the fields was about to be a reality.

"Patience, my son," Ivor said. "We must be certain everything is prepared before we act. The time will come, and it will be soon." Under his breath, he added, "I'm not getting any younger."

"How much of Ra'jhou will we be taking?" Ivor asked, despite knowing the answer.

"I won't stop until the entire realm is under my control," Tyrol responded. "Nilan won't be spared, nor will any of his line. We can't risk having sympathizers or false claims to the throne. Perhaps I will let you see to this."

Ivor smirked. "I'd be delighted. Maybe I'll start with the woman in my chambers."

Tyrol waved dismissively. "You may do what you wish with her once the war has begun. I care not. For now, though, she must remain safe and in communication with her family. They must believe she is well treated and content in her new home. We can't have Nilan thinking he needs to mount a rescue." Tyrol laughed quietly at the thought. He knew the Ra'jhouan army was substandard, and he intended to exploit that weakness.

* * * * *

Aubriana stood on her balcony, staring out over the sea. Her husband had visited her bed in the night, but there had been no sign of romance. Without a word, he had performed his duties while she fought back her tears. Her dreams of having a loving husband had been childish. Reality came crashing down on her as he left her room. Their marriage was doomed, and her future was uncertain. With luck, she would soon become pregnant and give birth to a male heir, which might bring a smile to her husband's face. Perhaps then he would appreciate her.

"My lady," Shala said as she approached the princess. "Your ladies in waiting are here."

"I haven't chosen any," Aubriana responded, wrinkling her brow. With a sigh, she realized she would not be given a choice in the matter. A queen of Ra'jhou would choose her own court, but the princess of Na'zora would get what she was given. "Put a smile on your face, Shala," she said. "Let us have a cheerful first meeting."

Holding her head high, Aubriana strode inside to her sitting room. Seven young ladies dressed in blue satin curtsied before her. "Welcome," she said. "I hope to know each of you well, and I hope we may all know friendship." If her husband would not show her affection, she would instead strive for companionship among these ladies. Perhaps some of them would become true friends. It was her only chance for a happy life in her new surroundings.

Shala handed Aubriana the embroidery she had worked on in the carriage. It featured a bright red rose with deep green leaves. The image gave Aubriana hope, and she smiled as she looked upon it. "I would like my ladies to wear red roses pinned to their bodices," she declared. She may not have had a say in choosing her ladies, but she would tell them how to dress and what duties to perform.

The ladies looked to one another and smiled. Apparently, the princess's first command had pleased them. They took their places on cushions around Aubriana's high-backed chair.

"Tell me stories of this land," Aubriana said. With a shy smile, she added, "Romantic ones."

The ladies giggled at first, but one of them finally spoke. "I will tell you the tale of a knight and the maiden who stole his heart."

Setting her embroidery aside, Aubriana leaned her head on her hand. "I would love to hear it," she said. Tales of love would have to fill the void her unhappy marriage had created. Though the previous day had brought nothing but disappointment, today brought her hope for the future.

Chapter 6

Four months passed as Efren and Ryshel enjoyed the freedom that came along with their marriage. Ryshel was delighted that her husband had proved to be a kind-hearted man, and they frequently discussed everything from history to politics. Though women in Ra'jhou were not typically expected to be educated beyond pleasing their husbands, Efren had given Ryshel credit for her sharp mind. She had not spent her formative years in frivolity. Learning about government and the lands around her had been a favorite pastime. Those conversations with her husband made her feel appreciated, not only as a woman but as an equal.

Efren had prospered as well these past few months. Despite his father's insistence that he would never learn to ride a horse, Efren had done so with his wife at his side. Her affinity for riding had sparked something inside him that he had never before considered. Upon hearing her description of the freedom she felt on a horse, he knew he must try it. Today, he sat atop a chestnut thoroughbred whose handlers had taught him to follow a specific path. Normally, Ryshel would accompany him, but she had awoken with some discomfort and insisted he go on ahead.

The songs of various birds filled his ears, interrupted only by the footfalls of his horse. The air smelled of freedom as he moved beneath the canopy of trees. Efren smiled to himself, glad that Ryshel had suggested he learn to ride. She was convinced he could do anything a sighted person could do, and he appreciated having her support.

As he neared the house, he heard his wife's voice in the distance. Though he could not make out the words, he could tell she was excited. With a slight nudge, he asked the horse to walk faster.

"Welcome home," Ryshel said as he approached.

Climbing down from the horse, he replied, "Are you feeling better?"

With a laugh, she said, "I'm wonderful, simply wonderful. I'm with child." She stepped forward and wrapped her arms around Efren.

Squeezing her tightly, he said, "A child? Already?"

"You are pleased, are you not?" she asked, slightly concerned. Though they were still newlyweds, she hoped the news would please him.

"I'm overjoyed," he responded, tears filling his eyes. "I love you." He took her in his arms once again and kissed her lips. "Is there anything you need?"

"My maidservants will see to my needs," she replied, blushing slightly. "Though, I might invite my mother to stay for a while. It would be a comfort to have her near."

"Of course," he replied. "Does this mean you won't be able to ride?"

"At least not until the baby is here," she replied. She knew it also meant a temporary reprieve from wearing corsets, and the thought pleased her. Despite the morning sickness, she intended to enjoy every moment of her pregnancy.

Returning inside the house, she decided to compose a letter to Aubriana. There had been only one letter from the princess since her wedding, and it had contained little information. Aubriana had simply stated that she was well and hoping to fit in among Na'zora's people. She had not mentioned Prince Ivor in any fashion, leading Ryshel to worry for her sister-in-law. Most brides would write at least a few words of their husband, but Aubriana had remained silent on the subject. Perhaps news of Ryshel's pregnancy would bring her some cheer.

Dearest Aubriana,

I hope this letter finds you well and in good spirits. Your brother and I have exciting news that we wish to share. I am with child, and we are overjoyed. Life in the country has proved to suit both of us well. There is never a dull day, and the weather has, for the most part, been beautiful. I hope the Na'zoran climate is agreeing with you, and I hope you and Prince Ivor are getting along well together. I would dearly love to see the ocean and hope to visit you someday. You are always welcome here, my sister, should you ever wish to return and stay awhile.

Much love,
Ryshel

Ryshel tapped the feathered end of her quill against the writing desk as she stared out the window. Perhaps her letter was too vague. Should she ask outright if the prince was cruel to Aubriana? Would it be appropriate? The two had met only briefly, but Ryshel felt a strong bond with her sister–in–law. Efren spoke of her often, as the two had been good friends growing up. Though their paths had been quite different, they had visited each other often, engaging in childish daydreams together. From Efren's descriptions, Ryshel knew Aubriana to have a kind spirit, and she hoped that spirit was not being crushed. After all, the princess had no one but her maid to remind her of her past. Her entire world had changed in an instant, and her current situation was something of a mystery.

Leaving the letter on the desk, Ryshel rose and approached the window. She had a clear view of the stables from this room, and she observed as Efren handed the reins of his horse to the handler. His smile was genuine as he turned and headed back to the house. Ryshel herself had overseen the servants as they installed various posts with bits of twine between them. Efren could navigate a large portion of the grounds with ease, unaided by a servant. His lack of freedom within the castle had been a sort of punishment. Here was a man wholly capable of moving about on his own, but he had been locked away at his father's insistence. *Never again,* Ryshel thought. *He is free now, and the king's wishes are irrelevant.*

Ryshel laid her hands over her belly and closed her eyes as the sun's rays warmed her face. Returning to her desk, she folded the letter and sealed it with red wax. If Aubriana's next letter was too vague, Ryshel would write again with less subtlety. Her own marriage was full of joy, and she would do anything in her power to ensure the same happiness for her sister.

Chapter 7

The sun shone brightly in the autumn sky as Efren and Ryshel sat in their garden having tea. The air of the countryside was fresh and clean, filling their lungs with its purity. Ryshel read aloud a tale of adventure in a land of magic, while Efren imagined what it must be like to cast such powerful spells. Often, he would interrupt her reading with a question she could not answer.

"Does mage lightning leave behind a scent? Surely it burns all it touches," he commented.

With a laugh, Ryshel replied, "I'm afraid I can't answer that one either."

"What it must be like to be a sorcerer," he said. Sitting forward he asked, "Have you ever met one?"

"No," she replied. "For that matter, I've never met an elf."

"It isn't only elves who can wield magic," he replied. "Humans are capable as well."

"I've never met such a person," she said. With mischief in her voice, she asked, "Or have I?"

Efren laughed. "If you're referring to me, then I must disappoint you. Had I the opportunity to learn, though, I would gladly take it."

"Perhaps you should write to the elves of the islands," she suggested. "They might send a tutor."

"For myself, they would decline," he said. "I've read of their teachings, and one must start training at a young age in order to unlock the power inside. It is said a human must be born with certain abilities, which I lack."

"Perhaps for the baby," Ryshel replied.

Efren laughed. "Perhaps."

In a more serious tone, she asked, "Is it your lack of vision that precludes you from learning?"

"I could not say," he replied. "All I've read is that there are specific signs that can be detected only by a master sorcerer. There are none of those in Ra'jhou."

"Let's send for one after our child is born," she said. Though she did not truly believe her child was destined to be a sorcerer, she wanted to give her husband the chance to meet one. It would bring him joy, and that was reason enough for her.

"Please continue the story," Efren said. "Forgive me for interrupting so often."

Ryshel turned back to her book and began reading once more. As the story progressed, Efren shifted excitedly in his seat, suppressing the urge to cut in at key points. Finally, Ryshel stopped to allow a few moments of discussion.

"I can see you're bursting to speak," she said. "Go ahead."

Before Efren could speak, a servant approached and interrupted them. "My lord, there is a visitor from the court." The servant bowed before taking his leave, and another young man approached.

Ryshel set aside the book she was reading and observed the young man's expression. It was plain that the news was not good. His eyes were downturned, his posture defeated. Clearly, something terrible had occurred. Her mind immediately went to thoughts of war with Na'zora. There had been little word from their king since Aubriana's marriage. Perhaps she had not been a high enough price to avoid an invasion.

Bowing, the servant said, "Your Highness, I come bearing sad news. The king took ill three days ago and died just this past night."

Startled, Efren bolted forward in his chair where he had been relaxing. "What illness?" he asked. "Is the queen in good health? And Gannon?"

Ryshel took his hand and squeezed it, hoping the answers to his questions would bring better news.

"They are well, Your Highness," the servant replied. "Prince Gannon is preparing for coronation tomorrow morning. The sickness that took the king is not known. He was racked with fever and convulsions. I regret to say his passing was not a peaceful one."

Efren's eyes filled with tears. The king had been a poor excuse for a father where he was concerned. He had lavished attention on Gannon, but he rarely had anything to do with Efren. Since Nilan saw his son as broken, Efren had not been considered worthy of the king's affection. They came together only during court functions despite having lived in the same castle for more than twenty years. He could not recall his father ever visiting him in his chambers or saying a kind word. Their meetings were always out of necessity and never out of fatherly concern.

"I am so sorry," Ryshel said, kissing him softly on the cheek. She was aware of their lack of a relationship, but she could see that her husband was upset.

"We will have to return to court for a while," he declared, allowing his tears to fall. "Gannon will expect us at the coronation." As a prince, he knew his duty. Sorrow was no excuse to be absent from court functions. His father's funeral would be swift, and he was determined to attend. Perhaps he could be of some comfort to his mother. Surely she would have reason to mourn the king, even if his son did not.

Ryshel raised a hand to summon her maidservant. "See that our things are prepared for a trip to the castle. We'll need clothes suitable for a coronation and also garments of black. Tell the groomsman to prepare our carriage." She spoke softly, hoping not to trouble her husband further. "Should I write to Aubriana?" News of her father's death might come softer if it came from a trusted friend.

"Gannon will see that she's informed," Efren replied. His eyes still glistened, but the tears no longer fell. Any hope of proving himself worthy of the king's love had died years ago, but his regret still lingered. Taking in a deep breath to compose himself, he vowed to be a better father to his children than King Nilan had been to him.

Ryshel stood, taking her husband's arm as they walked back inside their home. "Will you be all right?" she asked, concerned.

"Of course," he replied, nodding. "I did not expect to lose him so suddenly, and it pains me that he is gone. He was my king, after all." As a subject of the king, he was required to love him. As a son, he felt only regret.

Chapter 8

Within an hour, the couple was prepared to leave for the castle. Efren climbed silently into the carriage, followed closely by Ryshel. Once the luggage was loaded, she signaled the driver to commence their journey. With Efren remaining lost in thought, her only company was the rattling of the carriage and the thunder of the horses' feet.

Ryshel was startled when Efren finally broke the silence.

"I wonder how my mother is faring," he said. "Gannon will not have time to comfort her, and her only daughter is too far away." Though his mother had shown him only slightly more affection than his father, she had doted on her younger son. Gannon, of course, would be busy with matters of state, leaving the queen with only her servants to lean on. Would she seek comfort from Efren at all? He doubted it, but he could no longer bare the silence. He could find no other words to commence conversation.

"I'm sure your mother is well tended to," Ryshel reassured him, patting his leg with a soft hand. "I worry more for Gannon. With the king's illness progressing so rapidly, he has had little time to prepare himself."

"Gannon is strong," he replied, "and he has been preparing for this his entire life."

They reached the castle grounds early the following morning. The serving staff had been outfitted in mourning clothes, and the mood inside the castle was somber. No one would be allowed to laugh or make merry until a full week had passed. Gannon's coronation would be carried out quickly, and he would have to meet with his council immediately following the ceremony. Efren did not envy his brother the task ahead. He was relieved to be spared the burden of becoming king.

After stepping out of the carriage, Efren took Ryshel's arm. "We should see to the queen first," he said.

"Of course," she replied.

Slowly they ascended a spiral staircase and made their way down the long corridor to the queen's chambers. To their surprise, the door stood open. Servants were running back and forth carrying various items.

"Not that one, idiot," the queen's voice sounded from inside.

Efren sighed and stepped inside the room. Ryshel squeezed his arm slightly, hoping to give him strength.

Nearing the queen, he bowed slightly and said, "Your Majesty. How are you, Mother?"

"Terrible," she sobbed. Her voice was hoarse from both screaming and crying. Looking Ryshel up and down, she asked, "Are you with child?"

"I am," she responded with a slight smile.

"Well, there's no danger of the child being born blind," the queen informed her. "Your husband was born normal. The doctors lied, but I know it to be true. I believe it was an infection that claimed his sight. It wasn't my fault." She walked over to a chest full of dresses and began sorting through them, throwing many of them onto the floor. "Not these!"

A servant rushed to her side to collect the fallen gowns. The queen slumped down onto the floor and buried her head in her hands. Instinctively, Ryshel went to her side to comfort her. Composing herself, the queen patted her daughter-in-law's arm and nodded.

"Are you preparing to leave?" Ryshel asked.

"Yes," she replied. "My son has seen fit to send me away. I am only too happy to oblige."

"Where will you go?" Efren asked with concern. He had never been close to his mother, but he cared for her well-being.

"To an estate in the east near the coast," she replied. "I might do some traveling at some point." Turning her attention back to her servants, her face became visibly annoyed. "Can't you do anything right?" she shouted. The girls scattered, attempting to avoid the queen's wrath.

"Will you stay for the coronation?" Efren asked.

"No," she replied. "It is to be a small affair, and my presence is not needed." With those words, the queen collapsed onto her bed.

Ryshel rushed to her, followed by the servants who had witnessed the spectacle.

"What's happened?" Efren asked. He heard the commotion but was unaware of his mother's condition.

"She's fainted," Ryshel responded.

"Should I fetch a doctor?"

"No, she's coming around."

The queen sat up and stared into the distance unspeaking. Tears rolled silently down her cheeks.

Ryshel approached her husband and quietly said, "I'll stay and tend to her. Why don't you go and speak with Gannon? Your mother will be all right. She just needs rest." Looking over her shoulder at the queen, she added, "In time, her wounds will heal."

Efren nodded slowly. He kissed Ryshel's forehead before stepping out into the hallway. There was nothing he could do for the queen now. Alone he walked along the corridor to his brother's chambers. It was easy to follow the stone corridors of the castle in which he had lived all his life. Though this was his first unaccompanied walk through the castle, he had no trouble finding his way. Casually, he touched his fingers to the stone walls as he continued through the hallway.

Gannon saw his elder brother approaching and rushed to his side. To Efren's surprise, he grabbed him and squeezed him tightly.

"It's good to see you," Gannon said. "I wish it were on a happier occasion." His father's sudden death had shaken him, but he had been groomed for command his entire life. He felt prepared to ascend the throne.

"I have missed you these past months," Efren replied. After a pause, he added, "Your Majesty."

"Not for a few moments yet," he replied. "The ceremony will be small, with only a few dozen witnesses present. I have no desire to overshadow the mourning period for our father." He paused and stared at the ground for a moment. "Do you regret being overlooked for the throne?" he asked in a serious tone. It had bothered him over the years to know how easily their father had dismissed Efren's abilities. His blindness had not impeded his intelligence in any way, and Efren had been the one responsible for most of Gannon's political knowledge. His tutors bored him, but his brother had a way of explaining things that made it interesting to a young boy. In a way, he had been a more devoted teacher than the king. Though Gannon had spent the past few years involved in the King's Council, it was Efren who had a clever mind for matters of state. Gannon preferred military training and strategy.

"I have no desire for the throne," Efren said. "You are my king."

Gannon nodded, staring at his brother. "I will need you at my side," he declared. "You and Ryshel will come back to court and remain here. I shall name you my First Advisor."

Efren could not refuse the position, even though it would cost him the freedom he had recently won. His brother was king, and his word was law. Though his only desire was to live a quiet life in the country, he would now be forced to reside at court. Until his brother gave him leave, he would remain at his side. Once again he was trapped within the cold stone walls of the castle.

Chapter 9

"There couldn't be a more perfect time to strike!"

King Tyrol didn't bother to hide his excitement. "King Nilan is experienced, but his son remains untested in true battle. This period of transition is just what we need." He clasped his hands together, a wide smile spreading across his face. All of his plans were about to come to fruition.

"Good," Ivor replied. "My troops are growing restless. What are your orders?"

"Begin invading the border towns. Make sure there are plenty of survivors."

"Why?" Ivor was puzzled by the command. Surely dead citizens would send a stronger message than living ones.

"We need them to carry the message of our strength. They must spread fear to their neighbors. When they speak our names, they will quake with terror."

Ivor rolled his eyes. "How could I forget? Your glory depends on such stories."

Tyrol gave his son a scathing look. "Indeed it does. Each subsequent village we take will become easier. Citizens will flee rather than fight a hopeless battle." He paused a moment and added, "Make sure you send a strong message. Torture the town leaders, and make it spectacular."

"Of course, Father," Ivor replied. "We wouldn't want them thinking you've gone soft." He turned and strode from the room, leaving the king behind to bask in his own glory. Outside, the soldiers had begun preparations for a march. There were horses enough for the commanders, but the majority would have to travel on foot. The towns along the border were small, and heavy cavalry would not be necessary.

Ivor stepped inside the smithy near the palace. Hammers were clanging, and the air was darkened by smoke. The furnaces were working overtime, as were the metal smiths. At the sight of their prince, the men stopped hammering and bowed their heads.

"Is my armor ready?" he asked the largest man.

"It is, Your Highness," the man replied. Rushing to the rear of the shop, he approached a boy who was lazily polishing a piece of plated mail. Slapping the boy on the side of his head, he demanded, "Bring the prince's armor, you lazy little good-for-nothing."

The boy glared at his master but promptly rose to his feet to obey. In a flash, he retrieved the prince's items and handed them to the smith.

Inspecting each piece closely as he walked, the smith presented the armor to Prince Ivor. "Some of my finest work, my lord," he said proudly.

The prince looked it over approvingly. "It will suffice, I suppose." Though it was well crafted, Ivor preferred not to give compliments to those who were beneath him.

"You," the smith said, pointing at the youth. "Carry this for the prince." He shoved the bundle of armor at the boy, who struggled slightly under its weight.

The prince headed out, determined to speak with the commanders of the army's various regiments. A manservant spotted the prince and immediately rushed to his side. Relieving the boy of his burden, he waved a hand dismissively. The boy rubbed both arms, which were aching from the strain of the bundle.

Shaking his head, he realized there would be no payment for his services. Why should a prince tip a peasant or even acknowledge him? The boy trudged away, his head low.

Finding his officers in the armory, the prince was pleased to see them already dressed for battle. A map lay on the table near the men, and they appeared to be discussing the movement of their troops.

Ivor stepped heavily to draw their attention. The men stood and bowed to their prince.

"We will begin our march this afternoon," he declared. "Within two days we will reach the border, and my father has commanded us to raid the villages but not harm too many citizens. The leaders are to be tortured."

"He wants us to spread fear," the eldest commander said, nodding. "He's a clever man."

Ivor scoffed. "Personally, I don't care how many survivors you leave. A handful can spread the word as well as a hundred. The torture will have to be quick if fleeing citizens are to witness it. Drag the town leaders into the street and gut them before you remove their heads. Hold them high for all to see."

"The guts or the heads, my lord?" one man dared to ask.

"What difference does it make?" the prince replied. "Have the troops ready by midday." Turning to his servant, he asked, "Do you know how to dress a man for battle?"

"Yes, Your Highness," the man replied with confidence.

"Good. You may have the honor of assisting me with my armor." The prince dressed while his lieutenants dispersed.

Outside, the eldest man asked, "Do you think our prince will make a good war leader?"

A heavily bearded lieutenant replied with a laugh. "Not to worry. His father won't stay out of the fighting for long. Let the prince have his first experience of blood and death. It will do him some good."

"Let's hope he's listened to his father over the years," the old man replied. "I've ridden with the king many times through the years. He's a natural fighter. The prince knows how to handle a blade, but he's a poor leader."

"How do you know?" a third man asked. "He's never actually commanded anything."

"Exactly my point," the old commander replied. "By now he should have fought many battles. These years of peace have done us all a disservice. Our prince will likely charge in without thinking things through."

"Well, those years of peace are over now," the bearded man stated. "Battle has found us once again. Let the prince do as he will." The men parted ways, each with more vigor in his step than before. Battle ran deep in their veins, and they had felt useless in these years of peace. Now they would once again bathe in the blood of their enemy.

Still inside the armory, Prince Ivor felt his excitement rise as the servant fastened the buckles of his armor. Each second brought him closer to the battle he craved. His father's honor did not matter to him. It was time for him to make his own name—to triumph in battle as his ancestors had. He could almost taste his victory.

There would be little opportunity for his opponents to fight back. They would be too distracted mourning their dead king to worry about an invasion from the south. He would catch them unaware and massacre as many as he could. His father's wishes be damned. Every citizen he allowed to escape would be a symbol of his failure. His lieutenants would allow more than enough people to escape. His own regiment would be commanded to leave none alive.

Stepping out into the sunlight, Ivor's armor gleamed. He was eager for the battle and regretted giving his men until midday. Leaving now would be better, but the men were not prepared. Some of them were forming ranks on the palace grounds, but many of them were absent. The supply wagons were still being loaded, and the smithy was still buzzing with activity. There was nothing he could do except wait. The moment was so near, he could almost taste the blood.

Chapter 10

Pointing to a location on the map before him, Gannon said, "The invaders have stopped here for the time being. We must ride with all haste before they can advance farther."

"Will you lead this battle yourself?" Efren asked quietly. He feared for his brother's safety, knowing he had no true experience in battle.

"What else would you have me do, Brother?"

Efren shook his head and sighed quietly. There was no answer he could give that would please the young king. His mind was made up, and he was determined to fight alongside his men.

"We cannot let these attacks go unanswered," Councilman Faril said, striking his fist against the conference table. He was an older man who had experienced war with Na'zora in the past. Though his hair was gray and his face lined with age, he was strong and determined. "We must push them back into their own lands. Show them we are not a kingdom of cowards."

"I'm inclined to agree," Gannon replied. "They began this fighting. It is up to us to end it. I will lead my army personally. Let them see that Ra'jhou's king is not afraid to fight."

Efren swallowed hard but did not speak. He hated the thought of Gannon's first days as king being filled with war, but it was useless to try persuading him to stay behind. His blood ran hot, and he refused to be left behind regardless of matters at home that might need his attention. Nothing was more pressing than the attack on his kingdom. Once the troops rode out, all Efren would be able to do was wait for news from the battlefield.

General Willem, the man who had served under King Nilan, was eager to fight as well. He was tall, broad-chested, and wore a thick black beard. "I can have troops prepared by tomorrow," he said. "We should take back our lands and push into Na'zora's territory. Whatever lands we take we will declare them part of Ra'jhou. Let's show them who they're meddling with."

The king grinned and nodded. Noticing Efren's silence, he said, "What say you, Brother?"

Efren hesitated a moment before speaking. "We know little of our enemy's forces," he said. "Na'zora has been known to employ mages in their army. They may prove more powerful than you realize. I recommend caution."

"This one has no stomach for war," the general said, looking disgusted. "He would have you lie down before the Na'zoran king."

"I never said that," Efren replied. "I simply think it's wiser to know what we're dealing with before we rush into battle."

"You can let me deal with that," Willem declared. "It's not as if you'll be present on the battlefield."

"No, he won't be there," Gannon said. "He must stay behind and tend the kingdom while I'm away." He looked thoughtfully at his brother, the man who had his full confidence. There was no other who was better suited to the task of seeing to Ra'jhou's needs while the king was away.

A few of the councilors grumbled at those words, but no one spoke openly against the new king. They worried Ra'jhou would become a kingdom to ridicule if a blind man was left in charge, but they kept their opinions to themselves. The long history of war with Na'zora made them more inclined to support their king's decisions. With luck, the king would return victorious in a short amount of time. Efren wouldn't have the chance to mess things up too badly.

"We ride tomorrow," Gannon declared. "Dismissed."

The councilors marched out the door, talking among themselves. Their voices spoke excitedly, anticipating the battle to come. All were in favor of war.

Efren remained behind after the other councilors had gone. "Take care of yourself out there," he said to his brother. "We have never before encountered Na'zora's mages, not even when our father sat on the throne. They might prove far more dangerous than you expect."

Gannon looked upon his brother's worried expression. With confidence, he said, "Their mages are mortal. They will fall as quickly as any other man." He clapped his brother on the shoulder.

"Kings fall too," Efren replied solemnly. "Please take caution."

With a sigh, Gannon said, "Of course, Efren. Do not worry. Once we've shown Na'zora we are not easily defeated, they will yield and cease their fighting. They are only testing a new king. This will not result in an ongoing war, you shall see." He strode from the council chamber, leaving his brother alone.

Ryshel waited patiently outside the council chambers. She bowed her head before the king as he exited. "Your Majesty," she said.

"Sister," he replied. "Your husband will rule in my stead while I'm away. See that you take good care of him."

"Always," she said. Entering the room, she found Efren standing alone. Taking him by the arm, she asked, "Are you all right?"

"No," he replied honestly. "Gannon is a skilled warrior, but Na'zora uses magic. He is as yet untested against their kind, and it worries me."

"All you can do is wait and hope for the best," she said. "Concentrate on the work he has left for you, and the time will pass quickly. He'll be home before you know it." Her attempts to ease his mind had little effect. His face clearly showed his concern.

"I have no desire to rule in his stead," he declared. "I would rather he remained and sent soldiers to deal with Na'zora, but he is stubborn and believes himself invincible. That is a dangerous way of thinking."

"How would you deal with mages?" she asked curiously. She knew Na'zora had a special college where sons of the wealthiest nobles could study magic, but she had never heard what skills might be taught there. Nor did she have any idea how powerful those mages might turn out to be.

"I'm not sure, to be honest," he said. "I know that these mages have been trained by the Enlightened Elves. They are a race who guard their magical secrets closely. Their cooperation could not have been easily won. They are incredibly powerful, but I don't know if humans are capable of wielding the same level of power. For my brother's sake, I hope news of their skills has been exaggerated."

Efren's words hung heavily in the air. The Na'zoran mages were trained by masters of the arcane, and they were ready for a fight. They intended to take control of the Kingdom of Ra'jhou, adding its wealth and resources to their own. Efren wondered if it was possible to contact these elves for guidance. There must be some information they've withheld from their human students, and it might be of benefit to Ra'jhou.

"Your brother has trained in fighting his whole life. His councilors are seasoned veterans of past wars. For now, at least, let's trust in their abilities." Ryshel squeezed her husband's arm and kissed his cheek.

"I'll try," Efren said. After a pause, he added, "Would you draft a letter for me? I'm not sure I can trust the councilors who are remaining behind. I get the sense they aren't all that confident in my leadership skills."

"Certainly, my dear," she replied. "To whom do you wish to write?"

"A sorcerer," he replied.

Chapter 11

Despite hopes for a swift resolution, ten years of bitter fighting gripped the two kingdoms. Letters from Aubriana to Ryshel were still being delivered, but they came less frequently with each passing year. The princess was treated as a prisoner, and she was suspected of passing military secrets to her family in Ra'jhou. The accusation simply wasn't true. She was kept in the dark of all matters concerning the war. Her only visitors were her servants and her young son, Rayne.

Na'zora's forces outmatched Ra'jhou's at every battle, leaving Ryshel with no way to send the princess any letters in return. Still, she wrote about her own three children and how they had grown these past ten years. She spoke of the good health of both Efren and

Gannon, the beautiful weather of the mountain kingdom, and the king's lack of interest in marriage or the production of an heir. She avoided talk of the war. Every letter she had written sat undelivered inside her desk drawer. Ryshel looked upon them with sadness, wishing she could have the letters delivered. With the Na'zorans gaining ground within the realm, she knew it would be folly to try. The letters would surely be intercepted, and they could cause harm to Aubriana, who had already fallen under suspicion.

Efren had done well ruling in Gannon's stead, but he differed greatly from his brother in his opinion of war. Efren hoped to negotiate peace, but the council would not agree on terms. They were prepared to give Na'zora nothing, even if it cost more lives. Gannon was content to continue the fight. His idea of peace was slaughtering the Na'zoran king.

Instead of arguing with his brother or the council, Efren busied himself coordinating the movement of supplies that would aid the Ra'jhouan army. This included food, weapons, and medical supplies, which the soldiers desperately needed. The councilors were more involved in defending the outlying villages, leaving the supply lines unmonitored. Efren knew that if those items fell into Na'zoran hands, the war would be lost. Ra'jhou could not hope to win any battles with starving and sick soldiers.

King Gannon once again returned from battle to see to matters at court. He did so as frequently as possible, considering the ongoing crisis in his kingdom. Once the counselors had assembled, he stood before them still dressed in his battle armor. "The Na'zorans have been pushed back, but we still haven't regained our most southern villages. They are using them as bases for their army, and we must come down on them with force."

"We need more troops," Willem replied.

"There are none," Gannon admitted. "We have boys as young as fourteen signing up, but they are too inexperienced to be much use. We need trained soldiers, but there are no more to be found."

"We'll have to send conscription notices to the farming villages," Faril said.

"Farmers will be just as unskilled as the boys," Efren pointed out. "And that will leave our armies and our people without food. Who will produce grain and tend livestock when all the farmers lay dead on the battlefield?"

"The women could take over the farms," Faril said with a shrug. "It will make them feel useful." He cared not for Efren's opinions. Clearly the prince did not understand how to conduct a war.

"I think you will find Ra'jhouan women most eager to do their share, but they also have children to tend to," Efren replied. "You expect them to do the work of a housewife as well as the labor of a man. It's too much to ask."

"We are at war!" Faril shouted. Rising to his feet, he leaned in close to the prince. "No man or woman's path is easy. The other alternative is surrender, and I'm not ready for that!"

"No one is surrendering," Gannon stated calmly. "Farmers will not make good soldiers. They will serve as little more than targets for the Na'zorans. Food production is more important right now. General, can you appoint more men to train our less experienced soldiers?"

"Of course, Your Majesty," Willem replied. "At the very least, they will know formations and have basic knowledge of a weapon. They won't be proficient, but they'll do."

"Send messengers to all outlying villages and accept any citizens who are willing to fight. Bring all the criminals you can find. They don't get a choice." The king paused momentarily and looked at each of his councilors. "We must now discuss how best to manage our enemy's mages," he said. "At first they were of little consequence, but now they are growing in both strength and number. Word has reached my ears that they are now setting fire to some of our villages, using only their bare hands. Do any of you have knowledge of this magic?"

No citizen of Ra'jhou had ever studied magic, and the councilors looked from one to the other in silence. Efren alone had studied about the elves and the types of magic they could conjure.

"If the elves are indeed training them, then it is entirely possible they can produce spells of fire," the prince said. "They've had years to perfect the art while we've focused on the same tired tactics our forefathers used." At each meeting he had attended, the council's discussion of strategy consisted only of debating how loudly to sound the charge. Not a man among them had a new idea to share.

Councilman Faril scoffed at Efren's words. "I don't see you trying to learn magic," he said. "Our tactics have served us well. We would have lost the kingdom by now if not for our brave king."

The other councilors spoke up in agreement.

"I'm not saying those tactics don't work," Efren replied calmly. "I'm saying we have no prior experience when it comes to fighting mages. There has never been a need to defend against them, but now there is. We must figure out a better way of fighting. Perhaps we should try to form an alliance with the elves."

Voices rang out in protest, each councilman speaking over the one next to him. Ra'jhou was not friendly with its Wild Elf neighbors, and they would never agree to join forces. The Enlightened Elves were too far away, living on islands in the sea. Ra'jhou had only a few ships and no reason to travel so far.

"Quiet!" the king insisted. "My brother's idea has some merit. We do need a new strategy to defend against these magical opponents." He turned to his brother. "What do you suggest?"

"I cannot say how to take down their mages, but perhaps we can thin their army a bit."

"We thin their numbers every time we engage them," Willem argued. "What do you think we're doing out there?" He had no patience for a blind prince who could not stand and fight.

Gannon raised a hand to silence the general. "What do you suggest, Brother?"

"A diversion, perhaps?" Efren was thinking on the fly, but an idea came to him that might prove useful. "We can allow them to intercept a letter concerning the location of our supplies. If they think they can starve our army, they should take the bait. When they arrive expecting to find poorly guarded crates, they will discover instead that they are surrounded by our troops."

Nodding his approval, Gannon said, "That sounds like a good plan. We might catch them unaware. See to this, General Willem."

The general bowed to his king but remained silent. If the plan worked, Ra'jhou had a good chance of eliminating some of Na'zora's soldiers. Maybe a mage or two would be among them. Efren could only hope the plan would succeed. It was doubtful King Tryol would send a large force, so Ra'jhou should easily be able to outnumber them. Victory would likely be determined by the presence or absence of mages.

Before leaving for battle, Gannon took Efren aside. "Perhaps an alliance with the elves would not be a terrible thing," he admitted. "See what information you can find on the Enlightened Elves and whether they would be willing to teach our people as well.

Maybe we could come to battle with some mages of our own."

"I'll do my best," he replied. He did not mention that he had already been in contact with several sorcerers of the Sunswept Isles and Ral'nassa. So far, he had been unable to find anyone willing to travel in this time of war. In his studies, he had learned it takes decades for a human to master the simplest spells. It was obvious that Na'zora had been planning this for some time. His sister's marriage had never secured any kind of peace. It had only served as a diversion from the truth.

Chapter 12

Efren's strategy turned out to be successful. A sizable regiment of the Na'zoran army was defeated, thanks to his plan. Gannon sent word thanking his brother and complimenting him on his cunning. It was a small victory for Ra'jhou, and there weren't many of those to be found. The Na'zorans still had the upper hand, and their mages were still a force to be reckoned with. So far, the king himself had not encountered any mages. Rumors were spreading across the kingdom of their immense power, and the citizens fled in terror at their approach.

Efren sat next to Ryshel, anxiously awaiting his guest. After years of correspondence, a representative of Ral'nassa's Grand Council had agreed to meet with him. At first he insisted Efren do the traveling, but such a voyage was impossible. With Gannon constantly riding off to war, Efren would never have been granted leave.

A page entered the room, followed by a tall, white-haired elf. "My lord," the page said. "I present Master Uhnar of Ral'nassa."

The bronze-skinned elf inclined his head slightly. He wore an opulent, orange robe, decorated with swirling lines of yellow and red. His long white hair trailed freely down his back, reaching well past his waist. Standing nearly seven feet in height, he was the tallest person Ryshel had ever seen.

"I am most grateful to you for meeting with me, Master Uhnar," Efren stated. "I hope your journey was a pleasant one."

"Hardly," the elf replied. "I've come only because of your incessant letters. You've got the attention of quite a few high-ranking sorcerers, you know." Uhnar smirked and shook his head. "They were going to send a mere apprentice with a message asking you to stop contacting them, but I decided to volunteer my services. I could do with a little amusement."

Ryshel glanced at her husband, whose calm expression did not waver. "It is good of you to come," she said.

"Firstly, I do not converse with women. Dismiss her and we shall talk." He strutted to the fireplace and took a seat.

"It's been a difficult road to get him here," Efren said to his wife. "I value your opinion, but I fear I must oblige this guest. Do you mind stepping out?"

"I doubt I would enjoy his company anyway," she replied. With a curtsy, she exited, leaving her husband behind with the sorcerer.

Efren made his way to the fireplace and sat across from Uhnar.

"So," the elf said, "you wish to learn magic."

"I wish to learn a method of protecting my people from magic," Efren explained. "Our kingdom has never faced war against mages, and we are unprepared. There is little chance of our survival without your help." Efren did not wish to sound overly desperate, but he must impress upon this elf the seriousness of Ra'jhou's situation. If what he'd read was correct, they were an arrogant people who considered all humans inferior.

"It isn't possible," Uhnar said. "It would take too many years. Your enemy has been training for quite some time, and they are still inferior to us. Humans do not regenerate their own magic as we elves do. They rely on massive quantities of potions to maintain their magical stores. It's rather pathetic." His tone was almost humorous.

"Are you saying my people need not fear them?"

"Oh they're deadly, to be sure," he replied. "But they are far inferior to elven sorcerers. You should at least consider yourself lucky to be dealing only with humans."

Efren took a deep breath and tried again. "Is there any magical item you could supply that would help us? If we can't learn magic quickly enough, then there must be some other option."

"There isn't much." The sorcerer sounded bored. He had come to this land for amusement, and so far, he had found none.

At the risk of sounding rude, Efren replied, "Then why have you come? To mock us?"

Uhnar laughed and clapped his hands together. "I can see you are frustrated." He stared into Efren's crystal eyes and tried to see the man inside. "You care for your people, and these so-called mages are killing them. I personally don't see them as a threat, but that is because they are inferior in their training. I can speak to the Grand Council on your behalf, if you would like."

"Would you ask them to stop supplying potions to the Na'zorans?" If Efren could not produce his own mages, he might at least put an end to those of his enemy.

"No," the elf replied. "We do not supply them. For that, you would have to find someone on the Sunswept Isles who would listen, and good luck with that."

Efren was growing more frustrated by the minute. He had tried contacting the Grand Council of the Sunswept Isles, but they had ignored him over the years. It was disappointing to find out Na'zora's mages were not supplied by Ral'nassa. Still hoping to form an alliance, Efren asked, "Will your council send aid? Troops? Mages? Anything would help at this point."

"I said I would speak to them. That is all I can promise." The sorcerer slumped back in his chair, lazily twirling a strand of hair upon his finger.

"Do you know anyone on the Sunswept Isles who would be willing to converse with me? I have attempted to open talks with them for years, but my efforts have been met with silence."

"Now that is something I could do," Uhnar replied with a grin. He sat forward on his seat, placing his hands on his knees. "I have connections that might be of service. I can also advise you on how to speak with them more effectively." With a laugh, he added, "They are a fickle sort on those islands."

"Your assistance is most appreciated," Efren replied, wondering what price this elf would ask. There was little chance he had come this far out of the goodness of his heart.

"My assistance you shall have, Prince Efren," Uhnar replied. "As I said before, I've come for my own amusement. I trust you have accommodations for me? I don't plan to stay more than a day, though, so we shall have to work quickly. Have your servants prepare a room and meet me there." He rose from his seat, adding, "Have them bring wine as well."

Efren motioned the page to step forward. "See that our guest is made comfortable. Give him the finest room we have available and provide him with any refreshment he requires."

"I'm told you have many handsome ladies here at court," Uhnar said. "I hope I'm not mistaken in that?" He raised an eyebrow at the page, whose eyes darted back to Efren.

"Let us discuss business first," Efren replied. "My servant shall inquire of the ladies at court who might like to make your acquaintance."

"Splendid," he said. "Boy, make sure my ship is adequately supplied with wine. I'd like to take some of your vintage home for my friends to sample."

Efren nodded to his servant. If it cost him every drop of wine in the kingdom, it would still be worth it to stop the mages from attacking. He hoped Uhnar's help would prove worthy of such a trade.

Chapter 13

Sunlight filled Aubriana's chambers as she sat up in her bed. The window was open, and a soft breeze made its way lazily through the room. The fresh ocean breeze smelled far different from the mountain air she had loved as a girl. Though Na'zora had been her home for many years, she could not stop her mind from wandering back to better times spent in Ra'jhou.

Shala pushed aside the sheer bed curtains. "Good morning, my lady." Her voice was cheerful as usual.

Aubriana managed a half-smile. "Good morning," she echoed.

"I trust you slept well," she said, reaching for the princess's hand.

Aubriana sighed. Of course she had slept well. There was little else to do in her bed. Since the birth of her son, Prince Ivor had not visited her chambers even once. With the production of an heir complete, he considered his duties in her bedchamber to be over. He found pleasure in the arms of others, rather than in his wife's. Restrictions had been placed upon her, giving her little freedom to wander the palace grounds. She seldom left her chambers. On rare occasions she was allowed to attend court events, but those were infrequent since the kingdom was at war.

The highlight of her day was a visit from Rayne, her son. He brought much joy into her miserable existence. She would listen to him recount his playtime adventures, and her worries would be lessened. Her mind was ever plagued by thoughts of Ra'jhou, and the family she had left behind. If only she could visit, and take her son as well. Perhaps she would not return to Na'zora. With Gannon on the throne and her father dead, there was no one to force her back. If only there was a means of escape.

Shala readied a light blue gown for the princess to wear. "You'll look lovely in this," she said, stroking the satin.

Without warning, the prince burst into the room, the door clanging loudly behind him. Aubriana startled and raised her arms to cover herself. Though the man was her husband, she did not feel comfortable being observed in a state of undress. His presence felt no more familiar than any other man.

"The king demands you see him at once," the prince said coldly. "I suggest you don't keep him waiting."

"I wasn't aware he had returned from his latest campaign," she replied. "I shall be with him shortly."

Without another word, Ivor turned on a heel and exited the room, the door slamming shut behind him.

"What do you think the king wants?" Shala asked nervously. She lifted the dress over Aubriana's head and tugged at the laces on the back.

"I don't know," the princess replied. "I'm sure it is to scold me for one thing or another." The king was rarely in residence, as he was far too busy making battle arrangements to hold court. No doubt he wanted information about Ra'jhou. "He probably wants to threaten me with torture if I don't reveal my brother's secrets."

Shala gasped. "You shouldn't think such things, my lady. The king must know you haven't had any word from your brother."

Aubriana smiled, placing a hand on Shala's arm. "Don't worry. There's little else he could do to me that he hasn't already. I'm his prisoner, and I exist only because he has found no reason to dispose of me." Though her words and posture suggested bravery, in truth she was terrified. King Tyrol was a ruthless man, and any who crossed his path could expect swift punishment. Whatever he wanted, it was unlikely to be a trivial matter. He had never before requested her presence at court without an important reason. Word of a happy occasion would have reached her. This visit with the king would not be pleasant.

Shala immediately began twisting Aubriana's hair to secure it, but Aubriana held up a hand. "Leave it," she said. "He'll be even angrier if he thinks I kept him waiting for my own vanity."

Shala released the golden strands, allowing them to fall freely upon the princess's shoulders. With a nod, Aubriana headed out to the throne room, while Shala followed close behind. Aubriana approached the king with a polite curtsy. He stared at her, his eyes narrow, his expression severe. Ivor stood at the king's side, his arms held tightly behind his back.

"Did you or did you not send a letter to your brother that contained information about our armies?" Prince Ivor asked. He strode forward to stare into his wife's eyes. In his hand was a small piece of parchment.

"I did not," she replied. "I have no knowledge of your armies."

The king shook his head and waited for the prince to prove his case.

"I have a letter here written in your own hand." Ivor shoved the paper toward her.

Taking the page from her husband's hand, she scanned the writing. "This is not my handwriting," she declared. "I have not written to my brother since my arrival in Na'zora. I have corresponded only with my sister-in-law, and I have not done so since the war began." In order to send letters to Ryshel, Aubriana had entrusted them to the care of her closest friends. She trusted them completely. Neither the king nor the prince were aware of these letters, none of which contained information about the war.

"Liar! It is your seal!" Ivor shouted. Snatching the paper from her hands, he presented it to the king. "You can see, Majesty, that is clearly her seal on this letter addressed to King Gannon of Ra'jhou."

The assembled men at court began to murmur. Aubriana looked around at their faces, knowing she had already been convicted. There was no hope for a fair trial. It would seem her own husband had drafted a letter in order to frame her. She failed to see what such actions would accomplish, but she knew there was no chance of proving her innocence. Perhaps Ivor was planning to have her executed, though there was no reason to do so. He was free to pursue other women as he wished, and Aubriana maintained her silence on the matter. If he wanted her gone, all he had to do was send her away.

The king examined the red wax seal. "This is indeed the seal of Princess Aubriana. She shall be confined to her rooms with only one servant to wait upon her. She may have no visitors."

Aubriana felt a lump rise in her throat. "Your Majesty, may I still be visited by my son?"

"Certainly not," he replied. "You will not corrupt the heir to this kingdom. Guards!"

As she pleaded with the king to reconsider, two guards grabbed her arms and dragged her away. They forced her back to her chambers, shoving Shala inside as well. The doors to her chamber would be guarded at all hours from now on.

As the doors slammed shut, Aubriana crumpled to the floor in tears. Shala knelt, taking the princess's head and pressing it to her chest.

"Please don't cry, my lady," she said as tears ran down her own cheeks.

"My son," she said. "My son." Aubriana could hardly breathe through the heaviness in her chest. She was already a prisoner and had thought the king couldn't make her life any worse. How wrong she had been. Now she would be denied the one thing that brought her joy. Without her child, she had nothing.

Chapter 14

"My eyes have never beheld such a sight," Gannon declared, shaking his head. "Fire rained down from the heavens, unleashing chaos among our troops."

The war council remained silent, listening to the king's words. Na'zora's mages had been brought into full action, and they were quickly decimating Ra'jhou's ranks with their destructive magic.

"Their fireballs tear through lines of men without slowing. How do we counter such an attack?" Gannon looked around at his councilors, who were staring at the conference table, their heads held low. His eyes landed on his brother. "Efren?"

Efren shook his head and opened his mouth to speak, but no words came. After a moment, he said,

"Perhaps we could create a diversion? Draw their attention away from our main force?"

"How?" Gannon asked.

Efren scanned his mind but found he had no valid idea. What could possibly interest mages enough to convince them to leave the fighting?

General Willem scoffed. "He doesn't know," he said. "He's no fighter."

Gannon slammed his hand against the table and stood. "One of you had better think of something!" he shouted. "These mages are dangerous, and they must be stopped. Our survival depends on it!"

With a deep breath, Efren said, "I am working on something with the help of a Ral'nassan sorcerer, but things are not going as quickly as I would like." Master Uhnar drank more than his fair share of wine during his short stay, and he took half the castle's reserves back home with him. He also tried to charm all the single women at court, in addition to several of the married ones. So far, there was little benefit to be seen from his visit. Efren doubted that the elf was the most trustworthy person to depend on, but he could do nothing more than sit and wait. With any luck, Uhnar's contacts on the Sunswept Isles would prove more helpful than he had.

"Keep me informed," Gannon said, as if defeated.

Councilman Faril arrived late to the meeting, a somber expression on his face. With a bow, he presented a letter to the king. "A message from King Tyrol, Your Majesty."

Gannon snatched the letter away and sank into his chair. His eyes scanning the letter, he said, "It seems my sister has been found guilty of treason. He intends to punish her severely." Rising to his feet, he stared momentarily at the wall. Then, with a quick movement he kicked over the wooden chair, sending it crashing to the floor. "Damn him!" he cried in frustration. "I will rip his heart out if he harms my sister!" His face was red with rage. Tearing the letter to shreds he threw it onto the floor. "Saddle my horse," he commanded. "There is no time to spare."

"Your Majesty," Efren said. "We have no way of knowing if King Tyrol is telling the truth. You mustn't rush in too quickly."

"What gives you the right to tell your sovereign what he must not do?" Gannon was irritated by his brother's words. Though he was grateful to have him tend matters of state, Efren was a novice when it came to war. "This is a time for action, Brother."

"I only meant to ask you to be cautious. King Tyrol knows well that Aubriana has had no contact with us. I fear he might be laying a trap."

"I'm surprised by these words," Gannon replied. "You do not wish me to rescue our dear sister?" How could Efren possibly insist he take no action? Aubriana's life was at stake, and Gannon would do whatever it took to save her.

"That's not what I'm saying at all," Efren said quickly. He would do anything to shield his sister from harm, assuming she was truly in danger. There was no way of knowing whether Tyrol's letter was a trap. It was best to take caution and confirm this report if at all possible. Otherwise, Gannon might be risking his own life unnecessarily.

"Do you not fear for her safety?" Gannon continued. "I will not sit by while her life is in danger. King Tyrol is a monster, and he means to do her harm. Where is your courage?"

The disappointment in his brother's tone rang in Efren's ears. "I would not trade one sibling for the other," he said with a sigh. "She may not be in danger. After all, she is married to Prince Ivor and mother to Na'zora's heir. Surely even King Tyrol would not be so ruthless."

Gannon clapped his brother on the back. "Believe it, my brother. Our sister is in danger, and I will do what I can to save her."

"May I investigate the matter before you charge off into battle?" Gannon was not one to take caution, and it was common knowledge he would charge into battle on a moment's notice. Though he was a brave fighter, strategy and planning were not his strengths.

"Do as you like," the king said. "By the time your investigation is concluded, I will already have Aubriana back here safely." He strode from the room, leaving Efren in silence.

Efren rose and exited the council chamber. Slowly, he made his way down the corridor and stepped outside the stuffy castle. The air outside was cool against his skin, but the sun's heat warmed his face. He took a seat on the castle steps and sighed.

"Are you all right, my lord?" a passing servant asked.

Efren did not speak. Instead, he waved his hand, dismissing the servant. Moments later, the distinctive sound of horses rode past, their thundering hooves suggesting a large troop was already riding out in defense of Aubriana. Though he could not be certain she was not in danger, he could not dismiss the feeling that Tyrol was up to something.

The sound of trumpets accompanied the king's troops as he set off for battle. Efren rose to his feet, holding up a hand in farewell to his brother. The gesture went unnoticed by Gannon, who shouted orders to his men before riding off into the distance. Efren waited until all of the horses had passed, their footfalls fading away into silence.

Returning inside the castle, his heart grew heavier with each step. How many mages would his brother encounter this time? If he truly believed Aubriana was in danger, nothing would stop Gannon. He would charge into the mages as if they were simple soldiers. It could cost him everything. Efren struggled to keep his head high. His mind was in turmoil, his heart heavy. Whatever Tyrol was planning, Efren could only hope his brother would be able to fight his way through it.

Chapter 15

Hundreds of displaced citizens took up residence on the castle grounds during the king's absence. Makeshift camps were set up behind its stone walls, where the people hoped to find safety. Each day Ryshel walked the grounds, helping in any way she could. She fed livestock, brushed horses, and assisted in the castle kitchens. Her children helped as well, forgetting their stations as nobles, and placing themselves among the commoners. They learned some basic cooking and particularly enjoyed kneading bread dough. Ryshel took pride in their willingness to help. Her children would grow into fine citizens who would treat those beneath them with dignity and respect.

One evening, after a large group of displaced Ra'jhouans had arrived, Ryshel made a request of her husband. "I would like to take over castle management duties," she declared. "With the councilmen busy with the war, someone needs to see that the castle is being run efficiently. You are far too busy coordinating the supply lines and dispatching more troops to handle this new wave of citizens."

Efren was pleased that his wife would offer to share in the work of running a kingdom. There was already more than he could handle, and each night he went to bed exhausted. "I would be pleased to have your help in this matter," he replied. He trusted her more than any of the councilors and knew she had the kingdom's best interests at heart.

Thereafter, all affairs of household went to Ryshel for approval. Most Ra'jhouan noblewomen would not have considered taking on such an enormous task. They were expected to please their husbands and bear children, not manage an entire castle. It was expected that they would defer to their husbands in all manners concerning the home and money. Educating women in such matters was not a priority in Ra'jhou. If a woman could sing, dance, and embroider, she was considered well educated.

Ryshel enjoyed being in charge of the castle's affairs. There were hundreds of citizens to care for, and they needed new methods of keeping the area clean and safe. She saw to it that all farm animals were kept in pens, preventing them from soiling the grounds and spreading sickness. Also, she put dozens of men to work improving the castle's waste management systems. New canals were being dug to remove waste and prevent disease. So far, the citizens were healthy and thriving. Overpopulation was still a possibility, and Ryshel was constantly deciding where to put the newcomers. It was a demanding position, but one she enjoyed.

With Ryshel in charge, the castle grounds flourished despite the large number of people now housed within its walls. One afternoon, as she was inspecting the area, a slow procession of mounted soldiers came into view. They approached quietly, the king's banner flying on the wind above them. Ryshel's heart sank as her eyes took in the sight of King Gannon. His lifeless form lay upon a cart, drawn by his own horse. She stood frozen, barely able to breathe.

"I bring sad news, my lady," General Willem said. "Our beloved king has been slain in battle." He presented the king's ring to the woman who would now serve as queen.

Clasping a hand to her mouth, Ryshel's eyes filled with tears. "We must inform Efren," she managed to say. Turning quickly, she lifted her skirt a few inches to avoid tripping and ran into the castle.

Efren was seated in the council chambers, listening to his advisors argue over the location of a group of soldiers. The topic was unimportant, but each had his own opinion and was determined to share it.

The doors swung open, and Ryshel stepped inside. "My lords, I must inform you that King Gannon has been killed."

Silence filled the room, her words hanging heavily in the air. Efren swallowed hard upon hearing the news. His heart ached for the brother he had lost, but there would be no time for him to mourn. Whether he wished the position or not, he was now King of Ra'jhou. There was no other who had a claim to the throne, and his own sons were far too young for him to consider passing the title to one of them.

Ryshel moved silently to her husband's side. Placing Gannon's ring upon his right forefinger, she kissed his cheek and said, "Long live the king."

"Long live the king," one councilman said, standing.

The others followed suit, echoing, "Long live the king!" Each man made his way to Efren to kiss the ring and declare his loyalty. An uneasy silence followed as Efren found himself at a loss for words. He had loved his brother dearly, and his heart was heavy from the loss.

Standing, he took Ryshel's hand and pressed it to his chest. "We must get word to Aubriana," he said, thinking of his only remaining sibling.

"I've heard nothing from her for weeks," Ryshel replied. "It may not be possible to get a message through."

Efren nodded, determination filling his eyes. "Then we shall have to put an end to this war." Sinking into his chair, he whispered, "He and I disagreed before he left. I will never have the chance to apologize."

Ryshel kissed his cheek and gently rubbed the back of his hand. "Your brother loved you, and I know he held no malice against you. Brothers disagree at times. I'm sure he would forgive you without a second thought."

Efren nodded, knowing she was probably right. The best thing he could do for Gannon was to keep

Ra'jhou in one piece. To his advisors, he said, "I am not the man my brother was, and I cannot lead troops into battle. Nevertheless, I will strive each day to be a good king and to safeguard this land from its enemies."

In the back of his mind, Efren still regretted not being more supportive of his brother's last campaign. Was Aubriana safe? There had been no further word from King Tyrol on the subject. Perhaps Gannon's death was the result of the trap Efren feared had been set. There was no way to know for certain unless word arrived from Aubriana herself. Still, any letter from her could be forged, or she could be forced to say things that were untrue. Efren's only chance of giving peace to his brother was to bring this war to an end and negotiate the return of Aubriana. He could only hope it wasn't too late to save her.

Chapter 16

Efren was crowned the following morning, with Ryshel standing at his side. There was no crowd, and the general sentiment was somber. The councilors whispered to each other their doubts about Efren's abilities. Though he had been serving in a position of power for years, Gannon had always had the final word. Now they would have no choice but to listen to a man with no battle experience in this time of war.

Ryshel's role as queen was ceremonial only. A queen had no say in matters concerning the governing of the kingdom. She was expected only to supply Ra'jhou with an heir, which Ryshel had already done. With her duties managing the castle grounds, she held more power than any woman in Ra'jhou. She planned to continue her duties and to act as an advisor to her husband, if only behind closed doors.

After the coronation, she suggested, "My father would make a fine First Advisor for you, my lord. He has not been among the naysayers at court, and I have written him many times over the years what a wonderful husband you are to me."

Efren considered the idea. "Does he have much battle experience? I need someone who is wise, but also someone who will trust me. I have never been in a battle myself, but I have heard hundreds of stories involving war. I am not as uneducated as those at court believe."

"I know that to be true," she declared. "My father is a kind man, and he is fair and honest. He will serve you well, or you have my permission to dismiss him."

A grin spread over Efren's face. "You would give your king permission?"

With a laugh, she replied, "Indeed I would. Shall I send for him?"

"Yes," he replied. "It would be helpful if he could come right away."

They proceeded into the council chambers, where his advisors were awaiting him. Ryshel entered at her husband's side, escorting him to his seat at the head of the table.

As she turned to leave, Efren said, "I would have you stay."

Shock came over the faces of the assembled men. "Your Majesty, this is outrageous!" one of them declared. "A woman? On the council?"

Efren held up a hand to silence them. "She is not a member of the council, but I would have her remain at my side. I value her opinion as I do yours." He had no wish to shock his councilors so soon by officially making Ryshel part of the council. If they managed to save the kingdom from destruction, however, Efren had a few such changes in mind.

The councilman was obviously insulted, but he managed to hold his tongue. Ryshel looked upon the men's faces and smiled before taking a seat next to her husband.

"What news of the war?" Efren asked.

"Your Majesty," General Willem began, "your brother was slain by mages. He had not encountered them before, and we were not prepared to face them. They threw fire at us, frightening our horses. Once we were dismounted and our formation in disarray, the

Na'zoran cavalry charged us. King Gannon fell in the first wave, despite his valiant efforts."

A silence came over the council chambers out of respect for the fallen king. Finally, Efren asked, "By whose hand did he fall?"

Willem shifted uneasily in his seat. "The king's horse was struck by magefire. When he was dismounted, he was trampled. It is not the glorious death he deserved."

"Agreed," a dark-haired council member said. "We should record that he died in hand-to-hand combat, surrounded by enemies. His valor must be clearly documented."

Efren considered it for a moment. "My brother fought bravely through many battles. The manner of his life matters more than the manner of his death. We shall record it honestly—all of it."

There was no argument from the assembled men. A few of them nodded, accepting Efren's decision. Gannon had indeed been a brave leader.

Resuming the conversation, Efren said, "We must find a way to combat their mages. Undoubtedly, there is a way to defeat them."

"You have said yourself that we do not have the time or resources to train our own mages,"

Councilman Faril replied. "I see no way of fighting them other than what we're already doing."

"That strategy seems to be inadequate," Efren replied. "Were there archers among Gannon's regiment?"

"There were," General Willem replied. "Unfortunately, they were not ordered to fire until the mages were almost upon us. Had they loosed their arrows sooner, we may have rid ourselves of a few. We had no idea whether mages were among them until they opened fire. They were dressed no differently than the other soldiers."

"It would be unwise of them to stand out," the king stated. "They would be an easy target if they wore brightly colored robes."

"Then what do you suggest?" a bearded councilman asked.

"We will have to infiltrate the Na'zoran army. We need someone on the inside to carry out a secret plan."

The councilmen looked at each other, each hoping he would not be chosen for the task. The king's word was law, and none of them would be able to refuse the appointment should he be chosen.

"Your Majesty," General Willem said. "Let me find someone who is young and brave. Don't send one of these old fools."

Ryshel pressed her hand to her lips to stop herself from laughing.

"I wouldn't dream of such a thing," Efren replied. "We must send a brave soldier who would also pass as a noble. I have an idea that will require someone with quick wit, not someone with a quick sword. He must be tall as well. With luck, he will encounter no resistance."

General Willem wore a puzzled expression. Clearly, he did not understand what the king had planned. Whatever it was, he hoped it would work. "I will do as you request," he said.

"Once you've chosen someone, bring him here. The three of us will go over the details together." He had no intention of telling the other council members about his plan. They would not approve, and they probably wouldn't understand it. They preferred overt action to secrecy, but this was a delicate matter.

Chapter 17

Prince Ivor stood proudly, observing the village his troops had taken in the night. Most of the citizens had fled into the woods in terror, making the conquest an easy one. As a result, most of the buildings stood perfectly intact, meaning there was one less town to be repaired before Na'zoran citizens could occupy it. Of course, the war was far from over. There were still many other villages to be taken, and the major cities of Ra'jhou had yet to be touched.

The prince's troops gathered near him in the center of town, awaiting further orders. A single rider approached, his horse running with all speed. Ivor regarded it carefully, wondering if it bore a message from his father. No doubt, the king had some new plan and would demand he return home at once to hear it.

The messenger slowed as he approached the prince. Dismounting and bowing, he presented a sealed letter. "For your eyes only, Your Highness," he said.

Ivor took the paper, rolling his eyes. It bore the king's seal, so he knew what it would say. As he began to read, he realized this was not at all what he had expected. This was not a command to return home. Instead, this message contained fantastic news.

With a laugh, the prince announced. "King Gannon of Ra'jhou has been killed. The kingdom now lies in the hands of a useless blind man with no education or experience in war!"

The soldiers cheered, raising their arms high in the air. The war was sure to come to a swift end, thanks to the death of Gannon. All that remained was for Na'zora to march to the castle and dispose of the new king. There was a good chance that many of Ra'jhou's nobles would reject a blind man as their sovereign, and others would step forward to claim the throne. This division among the upper class would provide even more of an advantage to the Na'zorans.

"Ra'jhou's citizens will be in mourning, and the government will be in disarray," Ivor announced.

Once he gained control of the kingdom's lands, his father would surely place him in charge of Ra'jhou. Tyrol would never consider leaving his comfortable palace in Na'zora for a cold, drafty castle at the base of a mountain. Ivor, on the other hand, would be more than happy to take charge of the land. He would be far enough from his father to make decisions of his own. Perhaps, in time, he would lead forces into the mountains to conquer the dwarves. There were great riches to be found in those mountains, and Ivor was looking forward to obtaining them. A peaceful life without fighting was not something he desired. This war had only heightened his desire to fight, and he intended to do it for the rest of his life.

The men continued to celebrate, some of them dancing and singing. One man held a hand over his eyes, stumbling blindly around to mock the new king of Ra'jhou. While most of the soldiers laughed, one of them approached the "blind" man from behind, grabbing his leg. As the blind soldier toppled to the ground, he shouted, "Mercy for the blind!" His words were followed by thunderous applause and laughter.

Ivor shook his head, a grin on his face. "The blind king shall find no mercy from Na'zora! Let us make sure the citizens of Ra'jhou don't expect the war to end with the death of their king. We wouldn't want them becoming complacent. We shall take the large city to the north!"

The men shouted their approval and hurried to their mounts. The prince hopped onto his horse, raising his sword high in the air. "We ride!" he shouted, pointing his sword to the north.

For several hours, the company rode north until they came within sight of Ra'jhou's central market district. If it fell, this would be the biggest loss for Ra'jhou so far. Hundreds of men, women, and children lived in this city, which was also home to the majority of the kingdom's olive trees.

Prince Ivor commanded, "Form the line!"

His troops readied themselves for the charge. They would ride into the city, trampling all citizens in their path. Mages took their places in the center, which gave them protection from most attacks, though it was unlikely anyone would fight back. There were a few city guards to contend with, but no standing militia was present in this area.

"Charge!" Ivor screamed as they spurred their horses forward into the city

As the thunder of hooves bore down on their city, the citizens began to scream and panic. Women grabbed at their children, husbands reached for their wives. In the chaos, dozens of people were trampled, while others managed to flee to the safety of a large storehouse.

Prince Ivor shouted, "Hold!" The riders came to a stop, gathering near the edge of town. "Mages," he commanded, "burn the storehouse!"

The mages rode forward, approaching the building with caution. It was a simple wooden structure that would burn easily under their fire spells. Together, they began conjuring the flames, focusing their energy into their hands. One after the other, they unleashed fire upon the building, which quickly became engulfed in flames.

With a smirk, Ivor rode forward, followed by his troops. "Nowhere to hide now," he said. "There shall be no survivors to carry word."

As he approached the storehouse, he could hear the frightened cries of the people inside. He found it strange that they were not running out to escape the smoke and flame inside. Coming down from his horse, he approached the door. As he pushed it open, he beheld a grim sight. The people inside were already burning, their shrieks piercing the air. The extreme heat of the magefire had ignited vast stores of olive oil within the storehouse.

Glass containers burst, spraying oil onto the dozens of wooden crates as well as onto the burning citizens. The flames continued to spread more rapidly, ascending the oil-soaked walls to the roof. The weakened structure could no longer stand. In an instant, it crumpled, crushing the people inside.

As Ivor stood enjoying the grim spectacle before him, a heavy beam crashed down from aloft. It tumbled heavily to the ground, crushing him beneath it. His eyes stared up at the sky as his men rushed to his aid. It was too late. His eyes no longer beheld any sight.

Chapter 18

Word of the prince's death reached King Tyrol four days later. As Ivor's troops returned, they were not hailed as the victors they had hoped to be. They were greeted with silence and uncertainty.

Lieutenant Jak, who had served as right hand to the prince, stepped forward to command the troops and lead them back home. He stood before the king to deliver the grim news, his dark eyes full of sadness. "It was the magefire, Your Majesty, which brought down the storehouse. The flames were simply too hot." He held his head low as he spoke, refusing to make eye contact with the king.

Tyrol sighed and looked off into the distance at no particular spot. He clasped his hands behind his back and tapped a finger. "I cannot hold the mages responsible," he said. "They are far too valuable to condemn over this." How would he achieve glory without the mages? Dismissing them was out of the question, nor could he punish any of them. He had spent a fortune to have them trained, and they were the key to his victory. There was no other choice than to forgive the mages this error and move on. His son was gone, and he needed the mages if he was to succeed. "Young Prince Rayne is all that remains of my bloodline now," he announced. "You are dismissed until I am ready to make my next move."

Jak bowed low and backed away before turning to leave. Tyrol sat heavily upon his throne, contemplating the future. His takeover of Ra'jhou was going as planned, and soon he would control both kingdoms. Without Ivor, he would name his grandson as sovereign over the new territory. Ivor would have met with far more opposition from the nobles. Rayne was sure to be accepted more readily since his mother was a Ra'jhouan princess. Though Tyrol would be the one in true control, the citizens he planned to rule would accept and come to love the young prince. He was certain of it.

The question now remained of what to do with Aubriana. She had served her purpose as the "damsel in distress" and brought her brother riding to her aid. Now that he was out of the picture and Ivor was gone, there was no need to keep her.

Tyrol motioned a servant to his side. "Take a message to Princess Aubriana. Tell her she is forthwith banished from the kingdom of Na'zora. She has until nightfall to vacate the premises or she shall be executed."

"Right away, Your Majesty," the servant said before hurrying away.

Arriving at Aubriana's chambers, he shoved open the door without knocking. Startled by the servant's sudden appearance, Aubriana jumped to her feet. Shala approached the servant impatiently, her eyes scolding.

"How dare you come in here without asking permission? The princess is not accepting visitors."

"The princess has been banished. She is to leave by nightfall on pain of execution. The king has issued this command and expects her to follow it."

"My son," Aubriana said, her eyes pleading. "Did he give me leave to take my son?"

The servant shifted uneasily. "He made no mention of the child." With those words, he quickly exited the room.

"I can't leave without Rayne, Shala," she said, reaching for the maid's arms.

Shala looked to each side, searching for the right words to comfort her mistress. Finding none, she hugged the shaking princess close to her heart.

"I must speak to the king," Aubriana said, pulling away from Shala. Quickly, she turned and ran down the corridor to the throne room. Two guards stood at the ready, barring her entrance.

"Please," she said. "I must speak with King Tyrol."

Glancing at each other, the men slowly stepped aside. Aubriana swallowed hard as she opened the door and stepped inside. Shala followed a few steps behind.

"I did not request an audience with you," Tyrol declared upon seeing her.

"Your Majesty, I beg you to reconsider this banishment. Do not separate me from my son!" Aubriana fell to her knees at the king's feet. "I beg you," she repeated.

"Your husband is dead!" he screamed. "Rayne is my heir, and you have no purpose here. Now get out of here before I reconsider banishment and have you burned!" He kicked with his boot, shoving the princess roughly to the side. "If I suspect for a moment you have betrayed me to Ra'jhou, I will not hesitate to execute your son. Remember that when you are considering giving away any secrets you might know. I can always produce another heir."

Shala rushed to help the princess back to her feet. "Please, come with me," she whispered. "You mustn't provoke the king."

Aubriana sobbed. The king turned his head, refusing to look upon the grieving mother. Barely able to walk, Shala supported the princess's weight as they walked together back to her chambers. Gently helping her onto the bed, Shala busied herself packing the princess's belongings as quickly as she could.

A second girl arrived to help, but Shala said, "I need you to see that a carriage is prepared to take us back to Ra'jhou." With a curtsy, the girl hurried away.

"My son," Aubriana whispered. "My son." She wept into her pillows, her body quaking slightly.

Lady Bartin, who had become a close friend to Aubriana over the years, quietly entered the princess's chambers. She sat on the bed and leaned in toward the grieving mother. "I will do whatever I can to help you. I'll keep an eye on Rayne and write to you when I can." Rubbing Aubriana's shoulder, she added, "He will be safe. I swear it."

Aubriana sat up slowly and looked upon her friend. "Thank you," she said. Wrapping her arms around her, she squeezed her tightly. "I wish I could say goodbye to him," she said.

Shala paused in her packing to look at Lady Bartin, who shook her head. It would be impossible to bring Rayne here. The king would interpret it as an attempted kidnapping and have them all hanged.

"I shall give him your love," Lady Bartin promised. "If your brother proves victorious in this war, then you will be able to return and collect little Rayne."

"Gannon is a brave man, but there are no mages in Ra'jhou. There is no hope of victory."

Lady Bartin's heart sank. Aubriana had not been informed of Gannon's death. The grim news would have to come from her. "My dear Aubriana," she began, "your brother King Gannon was killed in battle about a week ago."

Aubriana pulled away from her, staring into her gray eyes. "Gannon is dead? Why has no one told me?"

"I'm sorry," she said. "I thought you knew."

Covering her face with her hands, Aubriana cried softly. Not only had she lost her son this day, but she had also lost her brother. She wept not for her fallen husband, whom she had grown to despise. His passing meant nothing. With a heavy sigh, she tried to focus her thoughts toward home, where Efren and Ryshel would welcome her. Efren had always been a clever boy, but even he wouldn't be capable of ending this war. Ra'jhou was far too weak. She would have to find her own way. Whatever the price, she would find a way to reunite with her child.

Chapter 19

It was early afternoon, and the sun was shining high overhead. In a rare moment of leisure, Efren and Ryshel walked arm in arm throughout the castle grounds. The air smelled of smoke as they passed by the smithy, where weapons of war were being prepared. The scent of ash and the sound of hammers served as constant reminders that the kingdom's fate was still uncertain.

As the pair approached the front courtyard, the wheels of a carriage echoed against the stone. Ryshel peered curiously ahead, wondering if her father had finally arrived to act as advisor to Efren. To her surprise, Aubriana stepped out of the carriage and quickly ascended the castle steps.

"Aubriana is here," she said to her husband. "She's returned from Na'zora."

"This can't be a good sign," Efren replied. "Take me to her."

They headed for the entrance, their hurried footsteps echoing on the stone path. When they reached the top of the stairs, Aubriana stood before them, her eyes full of sadness. Her appearance was disheveled, and she was plainly exhausted.

"My Brother King," she said, her hand against her heart. "My husband has been slain in battle, and I am sent away."

"You will always have a home here," he replied, reaching out to comfort her.

"Where is Rayne?" Ryshel asked, hoping the young child had not come to harm. She peered into the open carriage but saw only Shala inside, tending to the luggage.

No longer able to contain it, Aubriana began to weep. "They have taken him from me," she said through her tears. "They accused me of sending secret messages and would not allow me to see him. Once word arrived that my husband was killed, the king sent me away."

Ryshel rushed to her side, holding her tightly as she wept. There were few words that could be of comfort to a mother who had been separated from her child. Ryshel could hardly imagine such pain.

"I know not if I shall ever see him again," Aubriana sobbed.

Ryshel gently stroked the distraught mother's golden hair. "It will be all right," she promised. "We'll do whatever we can to help you."

Leaving the king in the safety of his servants, Ryshel escorted Aubriana to the bedchamber she formerly inhabited. The princess was distraught, and her tears continued to flow.

"We'll figure something out," Ryshel reassured her. "Efren is in charge of the war now. He'll do whatever he can to end it."

Aubriana laid down on the bed and curled herself into a ball. "They'll never let me see him again," she said. "They think I'm a traitor."

"Why would they think that?" Ryshel asked, taking a seat on the bed.

"They said if they found evidence of my betrayal, they would kill him." She continued to weep into the soft blankets.

"Aubriana," Ryshel said, "tell me why they would accuse you of such an act."

"My husband, Prince Ivor, and I never got along," she admitted. "I never told you, but he hated me. I was confined to my chambers on suspicion of treason, thanks to him." A wave of sorrow overcame her, and she buried her face deep into a velvet pillow.

Ryshel gently rubbed her back. "Efren will find a way. Give it time."

Her words fell on deaf ears. Aubriana was too distraught to believe the situation could ever improve. Her son was lost to her, and her world was in shambles. Eventually, her tears gave way to a fitful sleep.

Turning to Shala, Ryshel said, "You should go to the court healer and ask for some medicines to help her sleep easier. The poor girl needs her rest."

Shala immediately dropped the items she had pulled from one of the princess's bags and curtsied to the queen. Without a word, she hurried away in search of the medicine.

Ryshel let Aubriana rest while she took her position at Efren's side. A group of citizens living along the northern border had arrived requesting an audience with the new king. They bowed awkwardly before him, their common clothing standing out among the riches of the court.

One among them stepped forward to address the king. He was a tall man with dark hair who spoke eloquently despite his low birth. "Your Majesty, our village is under threat from dwarves. They have descended the mountains and taken up residence near our border. These are not merchants as we have seen before. These are miscreants who were exiled from their own homeland."

"If they have been exiled, then perhaps they have nowhere else to go," the king stated. There were far more threatening invaders to his south. A small band of dwarves to his north was hardly cause for alarm.

The tall man looked at the floor before saying, "Majesty, we fear they mean us harm. Every man among them is armed."

Efren sat silently a moment, contemplating the situation. Finally, he said, "Let us hope they have come in peace. I shall dispatch an emissary to converse with them and determine their purpose. If they are not inviting conflict, I hope you will welcome them as your new neighbors. Perhaps our two peoples could work together."

The man bowed again, not daring to argue with the king. With the matter settled, Efren moved on to the next concern. There were several small issues that required his attention: the treasury was quickly being depleted, the master of horse was not performing his duties properly, and several other petty complaints still needed to be heard. After several hours, each matter had been presented and discussed. When business was finally concluded, Efren rose to leave, followed by Ryshel. The sun had already disappeared from the sky, and Efren was weary from the day's work. Ryshel gently rubbed his shoulders as he sat on the edge of their bed.

"I tire of this war," he said.

Ryshel looked at him sympathetically. "Perhaps this new plan of yours will succeed and bring an end to it."

"Even if it succeeds, the fighting will not be over. We have already lost too much land, and we will have to fight to take it back." His voice sounded defeated, revealing his reluctance to continue the fight. "If only they would negotiate."

"Once you have them in a position of weakness, they may," she replied.

"One can only hope," he said, settling down onto the bed. Sleep overcame him almost instantly, his overworked mind insisting on much-needed rest.

Kissing her husband's cheek, Ryshel settled in next to him. Sleep did not come quickly for her. In her mind, Aubriana's plight played again and again. She could see herself in a worse position, should Na'zora succeed in taking Ra'jhou. Would they kill her and her children? What would they do to Efren? None of them would be needed; and all of them would be considered a threat. The people would be divided under Na'zoran rule if the old king and queen were still alive. All she could do was hope that Efren would find a way to defeat the invaders. Otherwise, she feared witnessing the deaths of her own children.

Chapter 20

The following morning, Ryshel's father arrived.

Duke Arden was tall and broad-shouldered, his face seeming younger than its sixty years. He was eager to lend assistance to the king in any way he could.

"It is good to see you, Your Majesty," he said as he stood before the king. "I thank you for inviting me to court."

"Welcome," Efren replied. "I have named you my First Advisor. Your wisdom is appreciated here at court."

"I am pleased to be of service," he replied, bowing.

Ryshel hurried to her father and hugged him tightly. "It's good to see you, Father," she said.

Arden beamed proudly, squeezing his daughter in his arms. "My daughter is a queen," he said. In all his imaginings, he had never pictured his own child on the throne of Ra'jhou. Though the deaths of the two previous kings had saddened him, he could not contain his pride. His own grandchildren would ascend the throne someday.

"Your Majesty," General Willem said, interrupting the pair. "I have brought the man you requested. Perhaps we may discuss your plan now."

A slender man of great height stood next to the general. With a few tweaks, he would look exactly as Efren desired.

"We will discuss it further in private," the king said, standing. "Duke Arden, you shall accompany us."

"Of course, Your Majesty," he replied. He followed closely behind the king, who led the men into a small chamber next to the throne room.

"Close the door and make sure no one is outside of it," Efren said. "Duke Arden, describe this man to me."

"He is taller than most men, standing a head taller than General Willem," Arden replied. "He is slender of build and has deep-set eyes. His skin has a heavy touch of the sun, and his eyes are blue."

"That should do nicely," Efren replied.

"This is Kal," General Willem said. "He is a fine archer and an intelligent man. I have observed my men closely these past few days and could think of none better to serve you."

"I need someone to pose as a mixed breed," the king stated. "Can you read, Kal?"

"I can, Your Majesty," Kal replied.

"Good. You will have much to learn, and quickly."

"I'm afraid I don't understand," Arden said. "You plan to disguise this man in some way? What is his mission?"

"Yes, he will be disguised," the king stated. "He will pose as a half-elf. With luck, he will infiltrate the Na'zoran army disguised as a potion maker. I intend to poison their mages."

The room fell silent as the men digested the king's words. The plan had merit, and it could prove a great success. Infiltrating the Na'zoran army, however, would be no easy task.

"Majesty," the general began, "this plan seems rather difficult. How do we get him past enemy lines? How does he convince them he's an elf?"

"If I may speak," Kal said, looking to the king for approval. "I once traveled to Al'marr, where ships from Ral'nassa often visit. They purchase gems there, and some of their sailors frequent the taverns. I know more of the Enlightened Elves than most men, and I have no doubt I can imitate one."

"Can you manage the accent?" the general asked.

"I can," he replied, speaking as if he were a native of Ral'nassa. "I have heard them speak plenty of times. I can explain away my ears with a story of my low birth between a tavern girl from Al'marr and a ship's captain from Ral'nassa."

A broad smile came over Efren's face. "I think you shall do nicely," he said. "You sound as if you've already been preparing for the role. General Willem, I will leave the details to you and Duke Arden. Get this man prepared and find a way to slip him behind enemy lines. They won't refuse his services, as they have great need of their potions. I have exchanged letters with Na'zora's original suppliers, and they no longer desire to remain involved in the war."

Willem was stunned. How could the king have possibly cut off Na'zora's supply of potions? Though frustrated that he had not been privy to the scheme, he chose not to ask questions. Whatever the king had done, it would only help Ra'jhou's cause. Now, the general had a new matter to attend to—getting Kal safely in front of the Na'zoran army.

"You are certain Na'zora will have need of this man?" Arden asked.

"I am," Efren replied. "The Na'zorans will readily accept his help. You have your orders." The king exited, leaving the three men behind. His confidence was high that the plan would succeed. Cutting off Na'zora's potion supply had been no small victory. If Kal could manage to poison the mages, the tide of war could take a dramatic turn in Ra'jhou's favor.

"You're sure you're up to this task?" Arden asked.

"I am, my lord," Kal replied. "Nothing would please me more than to rid Ra'jhou of its greatest enemy."

Willem shook his head. "Kal, you have no training in magic. These men may believe your look and accent, but they will never believe you are a potion maker."

"Yes, the king was quite short on details on that point," Arden commented. "Still, we have been given a task to perform, and we shall see to it. I assume there is a library in this castle? I haven't had much time to acquaint myself with the surroundings."

"There is a library on the third floor," Willem replied, his brow furrowed.

"We should start there," Arden stated. "We need every bit of information we can find on Enlightened Elves and potion making."

The three men found their way to the library, where an elderly gentlemen sat dozing behind a desk. The room was covered in a light layer of dust, suggesting few others had visited recently.

Arden cleared his throat, hoping to wake the librarian. "Excuse me," he said. "We are searching for information. I need to know about magic and potions."

The old man stared at him groggily, his expression slightly puzzled. "Whatever for?" he asked.

"It interests me," Arden replied impatiently. "Where might I find it?"

The old man rose from his seat and plodded toward a shelf at the eastern corner of the library. Sliding a tall wooden ladder along the rows, he pointed to the top of the stacks. "If I have the information you seek, it will be there."

Arden stared at the old man a moment, realizing that he would have to climb the ladder himself. Grabbing onto the rungs, he climbed to the top of the shelf. The librarian was correct. The top row was filled with books on the subject of Ral'nassa, the Sunswept

Isles, and specific topics of arcane studies. One volume in particular caught his eye—*Magical Abilities in Humans*. Arden smiled and nodded. "This one might prove useful." Grabbing the book, he tossed it down to Kal.

"I don't suppose there's one titled *Potion Making*, is there?" He grinned at the duke and raised his eyebrows.

Arden descended the ladder with an armload of other books. "I'm afraid not," he said. "Looks like we've got some reading to do."

Chapter 21

Shala walked casually through the castle corridors, hoping to avoid suspicion. *Act normally,* she told herself. *No one knows what you've done.* Arriving at Aubriana's chambers, she stepped inside, looking back over her shoulder only once.

Aubriana sat on her balcony, staring off at the Wrathful Mountains. Leaning heavily upon one hand, she took no notice of her maid's presence. Her mind focused on the scene before her as she tried in vain to drive away thoughts of her son.

"My lady," Shala said, her voice shaking slightly. "I have some news."

Aubriana turned her eyes to Shala, but her melancholy expression did not change. Whatever news the girl had brought would not be the news

Aubriana longed for. The only thing she wished to hear was that her son had been sent to stay with her. Nothing else mattered.

"You said I should keep my eyes and ears open for any information that could help you reunite with Rayne," the girl said. "I've heard something that might help."

Now she had the princess's attention. "What is it?" she asked eagerly. "What have you heard?"

Shala shifted nervously and took a seat near the princess. "I overheard a conversation. The king is planning something that, well…," she trailed off.

"Tell me, Shala!" Aubriana pleaded. "What is it?"

"The king wants to infiltrate the Na'zoran army. If you let Tyrol know about it, then he might consider you a friend. At the very least, he will know you weren't spying for Ra'jhou."

Aubriana looked deep into Shala's eyes, contemplating her words. "Shala, you must tell me everything you heard."

"King Efren, Duke Arden, the general, and another man who I do not know, met secretly to discuss poisoning the Na'zoran mages. It seems they want to send the tall man in posing as a half-elf. He is to offer his services as a potion maker."

Aubriana shook her head. "That won't work. The mages get their potions from the Sunswept Isles. King Tyrol pays a fortune for it." Her heart dropped, knowing that Tyrol would take no interest in such information.

"King Efren seemed to think he had changed that. He didn't go into details, but he said their original supplier would not be sending any more potions."

"You're certain of it?" Aubriana asked. She wondered how Efren could have accomplished such a task. To her knowledge, Ra'jhou had no relations with the Sunswept Isles.

"Yes, my lady."

"So, this man will offer his services, and the mages will be glad to have it," the princess said, thinking out loud. "They'll accept him eagerly, and he will poison them."

"I believe that is the plan, my lady," Shala replied.

"Efren must know this servant will be killed once he's discovered. The man must be expendable." In her mind, she began to justify what she was about to do.

"I didn't hear anything like that," Shala said. "There was no mention of how the man was to return once the deed was done." The maid had not followed the men when their meeting was concluded. She feared being discovered and having to explain why she was listening to their conversation.

"They didn't mention it because he won't return. They'll know who is responsible for the poisoning, and they'll kill him." Aubriana swallowed hard, wondering if this might truly endear her to the Na'zoran king. This unknown man's blood would not be on her hands, would it? He was doomed either way. "I must compose a letter to Lady Bartin," Aubriana said decidedly.

"It's the king you must inform," Shala replied.

"He won't take a letter from me," the princess stated. "He will think it's another plea for my son, and he will throw it away."

"How will we get the letter there?" Shala asked.

"Leave that to me," Aubriana replied. "I still have friends who will help as long as I meet their price." Hurrying to her dressing area, she stopped at a small wooden box and retrieved a golden earring. "This should be more than enough," she said.

Sitting at her writing desk, she took up her quill, but no words came. Was there a chance Efren's plan could succeed? If so, Ra'jhou could likely win this war, and she might then be able to retrieve her son. *No*, she realized. *Even without their mages, Na'zora's army greatly outnumbers Ra'jhou's. I must do this.* With a shaking hand, she wrote:

My dearest Lady Bartin,

I hope this letter finds you in good health. I have arrived in my childhood home, but I find myself missing Na'zora with every breath. I long to hold Rayne in my arms and tell him I love him. I hope he is not sad over my departure. I would have him be happy each day, even if I am not there to see it.

I have learned of a matter that might interest King Tyrol, if you would be so kind as to relay a message. I trust that he is wise enough to allow you to speak on my behalf. King Efren is sending a man disguised as a potion maker. I know Na'zora has need of one. The man will appear to be a half-elf and will arrive soon. Do not trust him. He intends to poison the mages to eliminate them as a threat. He must be stopped. I hope the king will listen to you, as this is a serious matter.

Sincerely,
Princess Aubriana of Na'zora

Aubriana shoved the letter away from her, stretching her arms across the desk. Her heart pounded in her ears as she tried to take deep breaths to calm her nerves. Was she doing the right thing? Would Tyrol believe her? Did this letter make her a traitor against her own family? Aubriana sighed. It was unclear which kingdom she should support. This place felt like home, but her son was destined to rule Na'zora. Would it be so bad if he ruled Ra'jhou as well? Only one man's life would be lost, and she considered him lost anyway. Efren was sending him to his death, so what difference did it make whether it was sooner or later?

With a quick movement, she folded the letter and sealed it with red wax. "Shala you must carry this for me," she said. Handing her the letter and earring, she said, "There is a servant in the kitchens who will know what to do with these."

Shala nodded and hurried from the room, determined to deliver the letter right away. There wasn't a moment to lose if the letter was to reach the king in time.

Chapter 22

Kal proved to be an eager student, and he absorbed the information quite well. With the help of his manservant, Efren had already studied the topic of potion creation and sent a stack of notes to aid in Kal's training. Arden found himself fascinated by the Enlightened Elves and helped Kal to adopt their mannerisms.

"These elves seem an arrogant bunch," the duke commented.

"Their sailors aren't so bad," Kal replied. "I mean, they do consider themselves our superiors, but they can be friendly enough. I admit I've never met any of their sorcerers."

"All of these illustrations show them scowling—the men at least. There are no pictures of their women."

"I doubt we'd find them attractive," Willem cut in. "Still, they'd be more interesting to look at than these books." Willem had not found the studying particularly exciting. None of the books had offered information on magical armies. The closest he had found were rules of dueling between sorcerers. It was unlikely Na'zora's mages would be using any of those.

For days, Kal studied the king's notes on potion making. Most of them centered on magic restoration potions for humans, but some of them spoke of remedies, antidotes, and potions that would increase a soldier's vigor. Kal wondered if losing its potion supplier had cost Na'zora more than just its mages' fighting abilities.

He spent so many hours poring over the material that he almost believed he could truly craft these potions. Most of the ingredients were unavailable in Ra'jhou, but he did practice using a mortar and pestle to crush various leaves, funneling flour into vials as if it were a delicate, magical ingredient, and eyeing his mixtures closely to make it seem he was being meticulous. He doubted any Na'zoran would be able to tell he wasn't actually crafting potions.

He prepared a satchel full of various brightly colored powders and leaves. Among them was a large vial of arsenic that he had tinted pale blue. On the vial, he marked a rune similar to a symbol he had seen in his studies. This vial was the most important item he would carry. If it was lost, he had no way of carrying out his task.

When he finally felt he was ready, he approached General Willem. "I've learned all I can," he said. "Let's do it."

Willem nodded approvingly. "There is a lightly guarded camp to the southwest where I believe you'll have your best chance of entering without a fight. You won't be able to travel on horse when you get close. In all those books, I saw nothing about sorcerer elves on horses."

Kal could not recall talk of horses on the Isles either. Still, he would be able to ride the majority of the way. He would need to walk only the last few miles.

General Willem presented Kal with the clothing he would need to wear. The king's personal tailor had crafted a dark green robe based on the illustrations Arden had supplied him. The cloth had to be expensive, as the poorer elves were not allowed to study magical arts. They were given the more mundane tasks and permitted to perform only the simplest spells. If he was to present himself as a skilled potion maker, he would have to look the part.

It was a few days' ride to the campsite, and Kal traveled alone. Companionship was impossible on a mission of such secrecy. The silence made each day drag on, and he found it difficult to sleep at night. Every time he closed his eyes, the same scene played over and over. He was crafting the poison that would rid Ra'jhou of its magical enemies. Each time, he was discovered before he could finish, and the guards would drag him away. He would wake just as their hands touched him, and he would have to shake the uneasy feeling the dream had given him.

If he succeeded in this mission, he would return a hero. Assuming he was able to return. The plan was to craft the potions and see that they were sent off before slipping out in the middle of the night. Hopefully he would be long gone before anyone discovered what he had done.

Finally Kal arrived within three miles of the camp. He dismounted the horse and rubbed its nose to say farewell. Turning it back toward Ra'jhou, he swatted its flank. Kal watched it run away for only a moment before beginning the final leg of his journey. It was now just a matter of steps between him and his enemy.

Kal felt confident in his abilities as he slipped inside the Na'zoran encampment. The task had been surprisingly easy. It seemed they weren't expecting anyone to walk into their camp alone. An army would have certainly drawn their attention, but one solitary "elf" drew no attention at all.

Kal stood perfectly erect, holding his head high in the air. With confidence he strode to the nearest guard.

"Who goes there?" the man asked, eyeing Kal suspiciously.

"A friend," he replied, speaking with his Ral'nassan accent. "I hear you are in need of a potion maker, and I've come to offer my services."

The guard nodded and grinned. "I was told to expect you."

A chill ran down Kal's spine. How could this man be expecting him? Neither the king nor the general had made mention of sending word ahead to fool the guards. He swallowed hard and remained silent.

"Follow me," the guard said.

With little other choice, Kal followed. Running would only increase suspicion. Perhaps a patrol had spotted him, and that was what the guard had meant by expecting him. He resisted the urge to panic and flee, but his heart was pounding in his chest as he walked behind the armed man.

The guard led Kal inside a tent where men were gathered around a map table. "I've brought an elf for you, Lieutenant," the guard said, grinning.

Lieutenant Jak looked Kal up and down before waving to dismiss the guard. "So you're the elf we've been waiting for. Come to make some potions for us, have you?"

"I have," Kal replied, standing tall with false confidence.

Without another word, Jak drew his sword and slashed open Kal's midsection. Kal crumpled to his knees, grasping at his wound.

Jak leaned down, raising Kal's chin with his finger. "King Tyrol sends his regards. Your plan has failed." With a second swipe of his sword, Jak removed Kal's head. Turning to the soldier on his right, he said, "Get a message to the king that the matter has been dealt with. The princess, it seems, was telling the truth."

Chapter 23

One week later as King Efren sat in council, a messenger burst through the doors. His expression was somber as he placed a rolled message in the First Advisor's hands. Bowing low to his king, he exited the room without a word.

Arden stared at the letter in his hands, failing to find his voice. After several moments, he finally spoke. "Majesty, it is a message from our enemy. It would seem Kal has been slain."

"Read me the letter," Efren replied, his face showing no emotion.

"To King Efren of Ra'jhou, I send you back your servant. His attempt to poison my mages has failed, and I will soon sit upon your throne. Regards, King Tyrol of Na'zora."

Efren drew in a deep breath and slowly let it out. How could things have fallen apart so quickly? What had given Kal's identity away? This was a bitter defeat.

Ryshel sat at her husband's side and maintained her silence. In her heart, she could already guess what had happened, and she intended to get to the bottom of it. Patiently she waited while the men discussed other matters of war. Once they had finished, she rushed down the stone corridor to confront Aubriana.

Throwing open the door to her chambers, Ryshel stepped inside. "You gave away my husband's plan," she said accusingly. "Admit it."

Aubriana lay unmoving upon her bed, her arm laying across her eyes to block out the light from her window. Her mind had been in torment since sending the message to King Tyrol, but she still felt as if there had been no other choice. "Yes," she replied in a whisper. "I admit it."

"Why would you do such a thing?" Ryshel demanded. "You have ruined what little chance we had for survival!" She was visibly angry to the point of shaking. All of her nightmares might now come true, thanks to the interference of the woman she had pitied and pledged to help.

Aubriana slowly sat up to look at Ryshel. Her eyes were red, her face pale, and her golden hair was in disarray. "I did it only to save my son. I hoped to prove my loyalty to Na'zora." Tears streamed down her face as she looked away.

Ryshel halted a moment, pitying the grieving mother. Would she have done the same for one of her children? Could she trade the lives of an entire kingdom to save one child? "You may have doomed us all," she said. "You owe your brother an explanation."

Aubriana nodded slowly and found her way onto her feet. Two maidservants helped her dress, and she walked beside Ryshel to the throne room.

"Your Majesty," Ryshel said. "Your sister has come to bring you news. You will want to hear what she has to say." She took her place in the seat next to her husband.

Aubriana fell to her knees before her brother. "Forgive me," she begged through her tears. "I have betrayed you."

Confused, Efren asked, "What have you done?"

Though choking on her words, she managed to say, "I sent word to Na'zora of your plan. I wanted them to think me loyal so they would no longer suspect me or my son of wrongdoing. Forgive me." She buried her head in her hands and wept. "I did it for my son," she said between sobs.

"Sister, you have traded the lives of my children for your own child's sake," he said quietly. "Na'zora will not spare my family when they arrive, and I doubt they will ever allow you to return there." He could hear her distress, but he felt no sympathy. His own sister had cost him everything.

Aubriana continued to weep. "I know it was folly," she replied. "I didn't know what else to do."

"How did you come across the information?" he demanded. "I told no one but Arden, Kal, and Willem."

"I sent a servant to listen in," she admitted. "The girl is innocent. She only wished to please her mistress. Please do not punish her. You may do as you wish with me." Doubting that any punishment could be worse than the life she was currently living, she resigned herself to her fate.

"What punishment is fitting for such a crime?" Efren asked, mostly to himself. This was his own sister who had betrayed him, and her betrayal might cost him his life. Execution would be the punishment for anyone else, but could he truly sentence his own sister to death? The idea was unthinkable.

"You shall be confined to your chambers," he said. "I will have to decide on a fitting punishment." He waved his hand to dismiss her, and she backed away. In truth, there was no punishment that could match her crime. Her actions might mean the end of Ra'jhou and everyone who Efren loved. Nothing could possibly make up for that.

Fearing what her husband might ultimately decide, Ryshel pleaded with him on the princess's behalf. "My love," Ryshel said. "I know her crime is severe, but I do understand her love for her son. She has suffered greatly since she was sent away from him, and I do not believe she is in her natural state of mind. Surely she did not realize the consequences of her actions."

"What would you have me do?" he asked. "Should I just forget about it? Do I give her the freedom to betray me a second time?"

"No," she replied. "I would only ask you to be merciful. She has suffered much, and she is ill."

Efren shook his head. "I have no intention of executing my sister," he stated flatly. "I am not unfeeling, and I know she suffers. Still, I cannot allow her the opportunity to betray us again. She must be placed under guard at all times."

"You are a wise and merciful king," Ryshel said, laying a hand on his arm.

"Summon the war council," Efren said to Arden. "We must revisit our plans. Our efforts to contain the mages have failed, and we must decide what to do next."

Arden bowed and hurried away to carry out the king's command. Ryshel escorted her husband to the council chambers to await the others. Once everyone was assembled, he informed them of Aubriana's treachery.

"We may all die as a result," he stated. It was time to devise a new plan if his kingdom was to survive.

Chapter 24

King Tyrol convened a meeting of his most trusted lieutenants. He was pleased that the situation with Ra'jhou's fake potion maker had been dealt with swiftly and cleanly. There had been no chance for him to harm any of the mages. Had such a plan succeeded, Tyrol's victory might have been in jeopardy. A vast portion of his resources had gone into training and supplying the mages. Now that he had no potion supplier, it was time to escalate the action. Otherwise, he might not have enough potions stored to see them through to the end.

"I have called you men here today to discuss preparations for a siege," he explained. "I know it isn't anyone's favorite type of warfare, but it is a necessary thing when your enemy is holed up in a castle, fearing for his life."

"We'll need to make sure supply lines are protected from our border all the way through Ra'jhou," one of the men suggested. "It might not be an easy task. It will take a large portion of our troops."

"Nonsense," the king said dismissively. "Ra'jhou's army grows smaller and weaker by the day. We can post scouts to look for any sign of our enemy's movement along the line and send troops when necessary."

"In that case, Majesty, we should use a portion of our forces to construct a wall around our camp. We wouldn't want Ra'jhou flanking us."

"That is unlikely as well," the king replied. "By the time we've reached the castle, all of their cities and villages will be under Na'zoran control. Whoever is left alive will be inside that castle. There won't be anyone left to flank us."

The men looked around at each other, waiting for the next suggestion to be made. It was clear that Tyrol had an answer for everything, and their input wasn't truly needed.

"Is there nothing else?" the king asked, surprised. "It seems I don't have the best military minds in front of me after all." Tyrol waited a few minutes, but none of the men spoke up. "Very well," he said. "I will need one of you to determine where Ra'jhou is getting their supplies. We must put an end to it now before they can stockpile a vast amount of goods. We wouldn't want the siege becoming overly long."

A red-bearded man said, "We've already taken out their central city where much of their grain is produced, so that should be a good start. We need to find where they get their meat."

"I have heard tales that they let their cattle roam the mountainside," a blond-haired man stated. "That would involve going behind the castle."

Tyrol tapped his fingers against the arm of his chair. "We can't risk going around the castle. They are not so weak that they can't defend themselves if we get too close. We will have to forget about the cattle for now. Meat won't last long in a siege anyway."

"We currently have no siege engines," a younger man said. "Is there time to construct such things?"

"We must begin immediately," the king replied. "I want every able-bodied citizen building catapults, towers, and at least one battering ram. We'll also need as many extra horses as we can find. I don't want my troops using all of their energy moving things about."

"Your Majesty," the red-bearded man said, "there is not enough wood to build more than two or three of these items at best."

King Tyrol slammed his hand against the table. "There is a vast forest on our doorstep! Cut it down!" He shook his head in frustration. "I swear, I'm surrounded by idiots," he muttered. "Do as I've commanded, and do not let me see your faces again until I have at least five catapults prepared to move out. Their construction is our top priority. I expect work to be done around the clock!"

With those words, the men stood and bowed to their king. They eagerly scampered away to carry out his orders. Tyrol watched them walk away and huffed. He missed the old days of battle when he rode with brave leaders. Those men were all gone now. In their stead, he had these wretches, who knew little of battle. When his history was written, Tyrol was determined to include how he single-handedly planned everything. Credit for Na'zora's success would be his alone.

Within days, the entire kingdom had ceased to produce anything other than timber. Even the artisans were enlisted to chop and haul wood. The forests surrounding Na'zora, which once stood beautiful and serene, were now wastelands of stumps and burnt foliage. Tyrol did not care.

As the first of his catapults was brought into view of his palace, he looked upon it in amazement. Stepping out into the courtyard, he ran his hands over the smooth wood which had been sanded to perfection. "This is a thing of beauty," he commented.

The engineer responsible for its design bowed before the king. "It's an honor to serve," he said.

"Load it," the king demanded. "I would test it to be sure it works."

"Of course, Your Majesty," the man said.

A handful of servants were enlisted to position the device, and a boulder was rolled in to load in the bucket. Once it was ready, the king himself pulled the lever, releasing the stone toward the ocean. It flew with marvelous speed, and the king clapped his hands as it splashed into the water.

"Excellent!" he cried. "Simply excellent!"

The engineer dipped his head and placed his hand over his heart, taking pride in a job well done. "Your armies will lay the finest siege Nōl'Deron has ever seen," he declared.

"Indeed we will," Tyrol replied. "I shall be remembered for the scale of it as well. Tell me, how many of these could we have prepared in a month?"

"At our current pace, I believe we could have a dozen, Your Majesty." The engineers estimate was generous, considering production of all other goods needed for war, including food, were at an all-time low.

"See to it then," the king replied. "I will rain chaos upon Ra'jhou!"

Chapter 25

Within days of Aubriana's betrayal, another Ra'jhouan city fell to the Na'zorans. A substantial portion of Ra'jhou's army had been defeated, with the majority of soldiers being scattered. The few regiments that remained intact had retreated north toward the castle. Some of them would never arrive.

Efren feared for the cities in Na'zora's path and ordered them to be evacuated. "Have all troops and citizens removed from the area," he said. "We will accommodate them here."

"But, Your Majesty," General Willem protested. "There are so many here already, and removing our army would be madness. We must continue to fight."

"We have already lost," the king replied, his head held low. "Do as I command."

"If we do not stand in their way, they will overrun us!" Willem shouted. "This is your kingdom. Will you do nothing to save it?"

"I am doing all I can," the king replied. "I will protect my people until the end. Do you have a better solution?"

"Stand and fight! Show them we are not cowards!"

"Their mages will incinerate what's left of our army," Efren explained. "I wonder, will you stand and watch them burn, or will you burn next to them?"

Without another word, Willem walked away. He was quickly losing faith in his king. Withdrawing when they should fight was unwise. Obviously, the king didn't know what he was doing when it came to fighting a war. Na'zora would see this as weakness and take the opportunity to advance more quickly. All Willem could hope for was to gather the troops at the castle and lead them in a final assault.

Efren stood in silence, listening to the general walk away. He had failed to find a way to combat the mages. Disrupting their supply of potions was the best he could do. With Kal's death, Efren's hope to eliminate the problem had died as well. Though he had searched at length to find a solution, he was no closer to learning how to combat the mages.

"Majesty," Duke Arden said, breaking the silence. "May I ask the logic behind removing the troops?"

"We must pull them back to help defend the castle. Ra'jhou will continue to march until they have taken every city and village we have left. Eventually, this will be the only place left standing."

"Then you've given up," Arden commented, staring at Efren.

"No," he replied, "but I don't want to lose more innocent lives. The people will be safer here on the castle grounds." With all his heart he wished his army was strong enough to put up a good fight. This was not the case, though, and he realized it. A new strategy was needed, and the only place left with strength was his own castle. If he was going to strike, it would have to be from here.

"Then you wish me to begin preparations for a siege?" Arden asked.

"I do," Efren replied. "We must gather all supplies remaining and bring them here. Make sure all citizens bring as much as they can carry from their homes. I'm not sure how long we can hold out, but we have to try."

"I understand," Arden said.

"The castle walls must be reinforced. Ryshel has worked closely with the citizens living on the grounds. Speak with her and find out who among them has experience in architecture or masonry."

"Of course," Arden said, nodding.

"There's one more thing," Efren said quietly. "We need to be able to defend the walls, and there aren't enough soldiers returning. I'd like to train any willing citizens, male or female, to use a bow. We need archers posted on the walls at all hours."

Arden's mouth dropped open in shock. "Majesty, your councilors will never agree to allow women to act as archers."

"I don't care!" he shouted, his face becoming red. "The women of this kingdom will die too if Na'zora succeeds. They have as much right to fight as the men." Taking in a deep breath, Efren tried to relax. "I am only asking for volunteers," he said in a softer tone. "I will not force anyone to do this, but I will not turn the women away. Any citizen over the age of twelve who wishes to be trained shall be trained."

"As you command, Majesty," Arden replied.

Arden made his way down the castle steps and walked among the makeshift camps that had been set up to accommodate the citizens. There were hundreds of people living in four separate camps. In a matter of days, hundreds more would arrive. Shaking his head, the duke thought, *They will be living inside in the cellars next.* Though he did not like the idea of living in the same building with common men, he would make do in this time of war. After all, the entire population was under the same threat.

Ryshel stood at the center of the northernmost camp. Upon seeing her father, she smiled and waved. "What brings you out here?" she asked.

"The king would like me to find you. We need to reinforce the walls, and he thinks you will know which citizens have the necessary skills."

"I know of only a few," she replied. "But I'm sure there are more than I'm aware of. I will find them and send them to you."

Arden continued to stand, staring out at the camp.

"Is there something else?" she asked. Laying her hand on his arm, she said, "Tell me what troubles you."

"I fear your husband has given up," he replied. "He has no desire to fight. He's pulling all troops away from the remaining villages, which will allow Na'zora an easy path here. They will march on us in full force, and we may not withstand the siege."

"Surely it is better to strike from a position of strength rather than let scattered groups be overrun one at a time," she stated. "I support the king's decision."

The duke nodded. "I'm not so sure, but you make a valid argument. Perhaps you can help with another matter."

"Of course," she replied.

"We need to train archers. I know a few soldiers who will make excellent teachers, but we need volunteers."

"I will spread the word at once," she said. "I'm sure most of the men will be happy to volunteer. Though there are no soldiers among the camps, there are many who would stand and fight."

"King Efren would like volunteers of both sexes, if they are willing." Duke Arden pursed his lips and looked away from his daughter. The idea of female soldiers still did not sit well with him.

"I will ask for any who are willing," she said with a smile. "Don't worry, Father. Ra'jhou's women are braver than you think. Mothers will not volunteer, but strong women who are stout of heart will jump at this chance to aid the kingdom."

"Just don't put yourself on the wall with a bow," he replied. Reaching for his daughter, he squeezed her tightly against his chest. She had always been a child of strong opinions, and that had not changed since becoming queen.

Chapter 26

More citizens arrived each day, but with guidance from Ryshel and Duke Arden, placing them went smoother than expected. Dozens of citizens had volunteered to train as archers, including several young women. They were thrilled to have the opportunity to defend the kingdom.

Masons and builders worked day and night to reinforce the castle walls. The paths into the mountains were cleared in case the people needed to retreat farther to safety. It wasn't an ideal plan, but there was little other choice.

Efren was pleased with the progress, and complimented his wife on her hard work. "You have done an amazing job for our people. I'm certain you shall be remembered as the finest queen Ra'jhou has ever seen."

Ryshel blushed at the compliment. "Any queen would do what I have if presented with this situation."

"I'm not so sure of that," Efren replied. "Ra'jhou has never placed enough value on its women, and even a queen might fear to step forward and take command." Drawing her near to him, he added, "If I am forced to surrender the kingdom, I will do what I can to ensure your safety and the safety of our children."

"Don't say such things," Ryshel replied. Pouring herself into her work was a perfect distraction from the realities of war. She knew well they may lose the kingdom, and even their lives. Those topics were not often discussed, and she hated hearing her husband despair. "We must remain strong," she said, squeezing his hand.

Sitting at her husband's side, Ryshel watched as a delegation of dwarves was led into the throne room. *They must be the ones the northerners were complaining about,* she thought.

"Your Majesty," Arden said. "The dwarves have arrived to give you their version of recent events on our northern border."

"There is war to my south already," Efren stated. "Have you come bringing war to my north as well?" He did not have the patience for a petty dispute. If they meant no harm, he would allow them to live in peace along his border.

A heavy dwarf with a thick brown beard stepped forward and bowed. "Most honorable King of Ra'jhou," he said respectfully. "My name is Pedr, and my people have come down from the Wrathful Mountains to seek a new home. We are refugees of a bloody civil war among our people. To my misfortune, I was on the losing side."

Efren smiled despite himself. Before him was an honest man, that much was plain to tell. "You have been exiled, then?"

"Yes, Your Majesty. We seek only a new home. We have no desire to harm anyone, and we would enjoy the opportunity to trade with your people as we once did."

"In my grandfather's time there was free trade between this kingdom and the dwarves of the mountains. The idea of such trade brings me hope. However, we are currently involved in a war, and I don't know how long this kingdom will exist."

"I am sorry to hear that," Pedr replied. "I would help you if I could. My people are highly skilled in weapons crafting, but we are few in number."

"How many have you brought?"

"Only a few hundred, I'm afraid," the dwarf replied. "We would make only a small army, but we will gladly offer our assistance."

The dwarves who had traveled with him chimed in their agreement before being hushed by the assembled councilmen.

"Then I welcome you," Efren declared, to the dismay of his councilors. They muttered among themselves, clearly unhappy with the king's decision.

"Come," Efren continued. "Meet with me privately. There are things we must discuss." An idea had come to him, and he once again had hope. Perhaps they could defeat Na'zora after all.

Ryshel rose to take Efren's arm, and accompanied him and Pedr to a sitting room.

"Leave us," the king said to her.

His command took her by surprise, but she obeyed, leaving him and Pedr alone.

"Could you get a message to your king?" Efren asked.

"Perhaps. I am an exile, but I still have connections." The dwarf observed Efren closely, only now realizing that he was blind. Such a king would never be accepted among the dwarves. He would be seen as weak. It intrigued him that Ra'jhou would follow this man, who was so obviously flawed. He decided Efren must be a man of great worth to be allowed to rule.

"I have a proposition for your king," Efren said. "One that I think he will find most beneficial. A silver mine sits unused on our northern border." Efren had an idea that would involve giving the dwarves access to it. Knowing of a dwarf's desire for precious metals, he hoped the king would agree to his terms. Silver's excellent magical properties made it highly desired among dwarven craftsmen.

Anxious to hear the king's proposition, Pedr replied, "You have my full attention, Your Majesty."

* * * * *

After hours of discussion and planning, Efren emerged to announce his decision to the court. "The dwarves will be welcomed along our northern border.

The towns nearby will offer them trade, and we will share the rights to the silver mine with them."

Murmurs spread all over the room as many disagreed with the king. One councilor boldly rose to speak. "Your Majesty, this is outrageous! We cannot give away the few resources we have left!"

"I said we would share," Efren said, correcting him. "This is my decision."

The councilman muttered something inaudible below his breath but once again took his seat. The others looked as if they'd eaten lemons, but none of them spoke.

Pedr fetched a second dwarf from his party and brought him before the king. "Majesty, this is Groot. There is no finer craftsman in the Wrathful Mountains. He can craft you magnificent weapons, the likes of which you have never seen. Your army will be better outfitted than any Na'zoran, including the king."

Efren nodded his approval. This new alliance with the dwarves might be the best strategy he had crafted thus far.

"I commend you, my lord," Ryshel said to him. "It's obvious your councilors are in disagreement, but I too see these dwarves as an asset. They will improve the strength of our army and give us a fighting chance against Na'zora. Well done."

"At least someone sees the wisdom in my decision," he said with a smirk. "I have set a new plan in motion. If it succeeds, Ra'jhou may be saved."

Chapter 27

"What is the meaning of this?" Duke Arden asked as he approached three men standing in a poorly lit corner of the castle. "Why have you summoned me here?" He was more than agitated by their note, which insisted he be present for an urgent meeting. If it was so urgent, why was it not held in the council chambers? Hiding in a dark corner was not an appropriate way to hold council.

Arden immediately recognized Councilman Faril as well as Idran and Pral. Their backs faced the wall as their eyes darted around, searching for uninvited guests. Faril motioned the duke to come forward. Shaking his head, Arden reluctantly obeyed.

"What's going on?" he demanded. "Where are the rest of the councilors?"

"Forgive us for meeting like this," Faril said. "We did not want to arouse suspicion."

"What could be more suspicious than hiding in a dark corner?" Arden asked, raising his eyebrows.

"This part of the castle sees little use," Idran explained. "It was necessary to find a place where we wouldn't be observed." The three men glanced at one another.

Pral cleared his throat and said, "We have a proposition that will succeed only with your cooperation."

Arden stood silent, awaiting further explanation. What could possibly require such secrecy? If these men had information that could change the war in Ra'jhou's favor, then it was something worth sharing with the king. Finally, he said, "Do you have a new strategy against Na'zora's mages?"

"This has nothing to do with the war," Faril replied. He looked over at Idran.

"We propose," Idran began, "replacing the king."

"This is treason!" Arden shouted. "You've all gone mad!"

"Please," Faril begged. "Keep your voice down!"

"You cannot seriously be considering this," Arden said. "There is war upon our doorstep. This is no time for treachery!"

"If King Efren were to suddenly be taken ill and die, we would have need of a new king—one who would prove a more effective leader in war," Faril explained.

"Nonsense," Arden replied. "A child would be left as king. Prince Melor is only eight years old!" Efren's eldest son would be the rightful ruler, and nothing these men said could change that.

"Yes, and such a king would require a regency until he came of age," Idran said.

"This is a time of war. The kingdom must not be divided over who will rule in place of a child. You three are wasting my time!" Arden could feel the heat creeping into his face.

"You would be the most likely regent," Pral said.

Arden stopped for a moment and stared at the men. They were right. In the event of Efren's death, Melor would inherit the kingdom. No one would allow a child to rule, and a woman would not be accepted as regent. With no other male relatives on the king's side, the queen's father would be the closest male relative. The duke was a nobleman with a good portion of land

and many supporters at court. Apparently, these men had thought this plan through.

"We cannot do this without you," Faril said. "There is no one else with such a strong claim to the regency."

"Consider this carefully," Pral said. "We're offering you a chance to serve as king. This is no small favor we would be doing for you."

Arden stared back at them with contempt. "You should be ashamed of yourselves," he said. "I'll have no part in this." He turned and stomped away, leaving the councilors behind in the darkness.

Though he tried to dismiss the idea, thoughts of becoming king crept into his mind. What would he do differently? Would he be able to hold the kingdom together? He shook his head. If he knew a way to win the war, he would have already shared it with Efren.

As he continued along the hallway, another thought occurred to him. What if Efren's death was all King Tyrol actually wanted? That would leave the throne open for the taking. One man could not hope to control both kingdoms, though. There was far too much land, and empires never last. The people of Ra'jhou would reject his rule and revolt. Tyrol couldn't possibly be in two lands at once.

Perhaps a deal could be struck with Na'zora. After all, there was a revenge factor to consider. Tyrol and Efren's family had been fighting for generations before the marriage between Aubriana and Ivor was arranged as a sign of peace. Obviously Tyrol had planned that as a diversion while he trained his mages for war. He might be willing to give control of the kingdom to a man who the people would support—a man such as Arden.

What would become of his daughter and grandchildren if he struck such a bargain? Ryshel was strong-minded and would likely never forgive him. Her love for her husband was true, and she would never forgive a man for betraying him to his death, not even her own father.

There was also the possibility that Tyrol would reject such a plan, and Efren might find out about it. In that case, Arden would be branded a traitor. His grandchildren would speak his name with disgust. No, he could not be a party to treason. King Efren was doing his best to protect the kingdom, and Arden was determined to remain at his side. If he wanted to effect change, he would do so from a position of honor, not one of disgrace.

With his mind made up, the only question remaining was whether to inform the king of his councilors' treason. They had not acted on their plan, they had merely suggested it. Arden doubted they would take any action, seeing as how he had refused the offer. There was no one else they could confidently place on the throne, so his unwillingness to join them should put an end to the matter. Until they attempted to act, they had not yet committed treason. Words were not the same as actions.

The duke decided it was best to remain silent but assign guards to watch over the three men. Efren would need extra protection as well, and his food and wine would need to be tasted before he could partake. At the slightest sign the men were planning something new, Arden would have them thrown in prison. This was no time for fighting from within. The kingdom must not be divided.

Chapter 28

"I doubt King Oge is going to be happy to see us,"
Darly said, looking over her shoulder at the
mountains. She wasn't looking forward to the arduous
trek back to her homeland. Since arriving at the new
camp, she had begun to feel at home.

"Queen Zella won't be so happy about it either, but
there's nothing else I can do," Pedr replied. "And
don't think you're coming with me. You've got to stay
here and take care of this lot."

The majority of the dwarves would be staying
behind at Ra'jhou's northern border. If Pedr entered
dwarven lands with more than a handful of
companions, it might be mistaken for an invasion.
Pedr had supported King Oge during the dwarven
civil war, but he had fallen out of favor with the queen.

Oge stood by as Pedr was banished, offering no pardon for a loyal subject. Now Pedr had the chance to serve a new king. Though Efren was a human, he was more respectable to Pedr's eyes than the current royal family of his homeland.

"Who's going with you then?" Darly asked, her hands on her hips. "Groot?"

"No," Pedr replied, shaking his head. "They're in dire need of his skills here. I've asked Geryl and Bor to come with me. They're members of the queen's own family, so maybe she won't be too angry to see them."

"What if she has you tossed in the dungeons?" Darly asked. "What am I supposed to do without my husband?"

"You'll just have to take over for me," he said, chuckling. "King Efren has already promised us mining rights. All you have to do is help build a new village here."

"Well, King Efren might not be king for long. Those invaders might take everything, including this silver mine." Darly had been visiting the small village that lay between the dwarf settlement and the castle. There was plenty of talk about the war, and she loved listening to gossip. She had picked up quite a few details regarding the king's abilities to conduct a war.

"If that's the case," Pedr began, "then we'll just have to find someplace else. From what I've heard, we won't want to be under the Na'zoran king's control. He won't be too keen on sharing profits from the silver, either." He shook his head. "No, if Ra'jhou is taken, we'll have to move on."

"Assuming you're in the dungeons, I'll be the one who has to move on." Darly crossed her arms. She hated the idea of parting with the man she'd spent her entire life with. During the war, she had worried each day that she might lose him. After they left the mountains, she thought those days of worry were over. They came to this land to start a new life—a life of peace. With Pedr going back into the fire, she feared what might become of him. Queen Zella did not forgive easily.

"You do whatever is best for these people," he said, placing his hands on her shoulders and turning her to look upon the village. Dwarf children ran and played, laughing as they passed by. Men and women busied themselves building temporary homes and preparing the land for habitation.

"This land is worth keeping, Darly," he said. "I'm a better judge of character than I ever was, and King Efren will treat our people right. If I can help him save his kingdom, we just might have ourselves a home."

Darly's eyes filled with tears as she embraced her husband. "Come back to me," she whispered. Grabbing a large leather bag, she helped him position it on his back. "I packed dried venison, pine nuts, and three loaves of bread I baked just this morning." She wiped at her nose, which was already turning red.

Pedr leaned in to kiss her and stroke her hair before stepping away. "I'll see you soon," he said.

"You'd better," she replied.

With a cheerful wave, he started toward the mountain, where his two companions were already waiting.

"All set?" Bor asked as Pedr approached.

"Yep," he replied. "Let's see how far we can get before nightfall."

"I sure hope you know what you're doing," Bor remarked with a crooked grin.

"Me too," Pedr replied, clapping his friend on the back.

The trio journeyed into the mountains with little conversation between them. There were many miles to traverse, and they would need to travel as quickly as possible. The air thinned as they ascended, and a chill entered the air. For hours they trudged, their feet sticking in the moistened earth from the snow melting high above. Luckily, they would not need to reach the summit. The king resided only about halfway up, in a palace carved into the mountain itself.

The sun was setting quickly, and light was becoming scarce before the men decided to make camp. "This seems as good a resting place as any," Pedr commented. "Let's get a fire going."

After building a fire and snacking on the rations they had brought, the men spread out their bedrolls and settled in for the night.

"You know," Geryl said before lying down, "that silver mine could support a lot more dwarves than we brought with us. Maybe we should see if anyone else is interested in joining us. They've had a while to see whether they're happy with the new king."

Bor shrugged. "That's not a bad idea. Unless we want to depend on the Ra'jhouans for all of our trade, we should at least try to win a few more allies while we're back home."

"We have to be careful," Pedr replied. "We don't want them to think we're trying to reignite a revolution. It's going to be hard enough convincing Oge to listen to me."

"You were his supporter," Bor reminded him. "He will listen. He might not act, but he will listen."

Pedr wasn't so sure, but he was glad to have Bor's confidence. Queen Zella was a powerful woman, and she may well refuse to grant Pedr access to her husband. Though dwarf women would not be permitted to rule alone, this queen held great sway over her young husband. Still, things had settled down some since the end of the civil war, and there had been no rumors of further unrest throughout the kingdom. All Pedr could do was hope that his proposal would be accepted. His new life depended on it.

Chapter 29

For several days, Aubriana did not rise from her bed. She refused to eat, and her body was showing signs of wasting. The servants had gone so far as to force-feed her in an effort to preserve her life. Ryshel visited her each day, hoping to bring her some cheer. She decided that a visit from her own children might put a smile on the suffering princess's face.

With her three children behind her, Ryshel slowly approached Aubriana's bedside. "I've brought visitors to cheer you," she said. Stepping aside, she motioned her children to come forward.

Aubriana lifted herself on her elbow and looked into the eyes of Ryshel's youngest boy. He was blond-haired like her own son, and his eyes twinkled brightly. For a moment, she thought she might smile, but the realization he was not her son hit her hard. Letting out a wail, she buried her face in her blankets.

Ryshel realized she had erred in bringing the children. They had only served as a further reminder that Rayne was so far away. "Come along, children," she said. The three of them followed her away from their suffering aunt.

Returning to her children's rooms, she sat near the window to think. What could she do to help Aubriana? What would she do to retrieve her own children? After a while, her mind was made up.

"Governess," she called. "See to the children. I need to have a word with the king."

She strode confidently to the council chamber and was surprised to find the king alone. "Is everything all right?" she asked.

"I know not," he replied. "It is far too soon to have any word from Pedr. For all I know, my new plan may have already failed as the last one did."

"Have confidence, my king," she said, coming to his side. Kneeling next to his chair, she softly kissed his cheek. As she looked upon his face, she realized her own plan was going to be difficult for him as well. It would require her to leave him for a while, and her heart ached at the thought of it.

"I must tell you of an idea I've had to help Aubriana," she stated after a few moments of silence. "It hasn't been an easy decision."

"What do you mean?" he asked, puzzled.

"I intend to leave for Na'zora, posing as a nursemaid."

Efren jumped to his feet, grabbing his wife's arm. "Have you gone mad? They'll kill you!"

"Aubriana still has friends there. They will help me. Once I'm in, I can secure Rayne's safety and smuggle him back here."

"You are a queen," he reminded her. "It isn't possible for you to do this. I won't allow it."

"Would you have me send a servant instead?" she asked. "Would you then have that servant buried next to Kal? I will not send another to certain death. Aubriana's friends will help me. If I'm discovered, they will use me as a hostage. Even King Tyrol would not be so bold as to execute a queen."

Efren's eyes filled with tears. He knew he would not be able to dissuade his wife, no matter what he said. "I have no doubt that he would give such a cruel order. We are losing this war, and he will kill us all if he can."

Ryshel wrapped her arms around her husband. "I am a valuable hostage. I will be safe."

"They will demand a ransom that I might not be able to pay," Efren replied. "They might ask for the kingdom. What would you have me do?"

"Give them nothing." Her mind was made up. No matter the consequences to herself, she was determined to reunite Rayne with his mother.

"You would leave your own children to save your nephew?" Efren asked, pleading. He could not understand her reasoning.

"My children are safe here, but my nephew is not. Our children have their father, but Rayne's father is dead. He has no one. I must go." Ryshel feared she might lose her nerve as tears began welling in her eyes. She could see no other solution, though she would miss her own children dearly. At least they were safe and warm in the castle. Their fate would match that of the kingdom, and with luck, Efren's secret plan would save them all.

"When will you leave?" he asked, sitting back in his chair. His posture showed his defeat as he rubbed his hand against his forehead.

"I will go at once," she replied. With a single kiss, she left her husband to prepare for her journey.

As soon as she reached her quarters, she sent her maidservant to fetch her disguise. "Bring me some of your own clothing," she said. "I need something that doesn't look too new, nor too expensive. Something plain and simple."

The young girl hurried away to obey while Ryshel removed her jewelry. Placing it carefully upon her dresser, she stared at the glittering gems. Knowing how little such riches meant compared to the life of a child, she was happy to put them aside. She would take on the guise of a servant and forget for a while that she was a queen. All her mind would be dedicated to the ruse.

The maid returned with a simple cotton dress. "This is the plain dress I wear on wash day," she said almost apologetically.

"It will do nicely," Ryshel said. As she pulled on her maid's dress, she realized it was more comfortable than the fancy gowns she usually wore. "It's not as bad as I thought it would be," she admitted with a laugh. "Thank you for your help."

She stuffed a handful of coins into a small leather purse, which she hid inside her dress. Bribes might be necessary, and she might require a nicer dress for serving as governess to a prince. There was no time to waste. She needed to leave immediately before she lost her courage. *The sooner I leave, the sooner I can return home.*

Ryshel made her way back to Aubriana's chambers. Strewn about on her desk were dozens of letters that had made it past the armies. *If these letters can make it, so can I*, she thought. These letters contained all the information she would need to find the princess's friends. *Aubriana's friends had better come through for me*, she thought. *If not, I'll never succeed.*

Chapter 30

After a tearful farewell to her own children, Ryshel was ready to set out for Na'zora. Efren managed to hire a small ship to carry her in safety around the coastline. There was no safe passage by land, as Na'zoran troops currently occupied nearly all of the outlying villages. Ryshel would go on horseback to the coast, accompanied by two members of the royal guard. A merchant ship would be waiting there to greet her.

"There is nothing I can say to dissuade you?" Efren asked as Ryshel prepared to leave.

"I have to do this," she replied. Putting on a smile, she added, "I'll be back with little Rayne before you know it." She had said the exact same words to her own children, and they had stuck in her throat then

213

too. Leaving her family behind was agony, but she could see no other choice.

Reaching into her pocket, Ryshel pulled out a small bit of parchment. "Give this note to Shala, your sister's servant. She will know how to get the message through to Na'zora."

Efren took the paper and handed it to his manservant. Taking Ryshel in his arms, he squeezed her tightly, wishing he did not have to let go. "I love you," he said, his eyes filling with tears. "There is nothing else left to say."

Tears rolled silently down Ryshel's cheeks as she kissed her husband one last time. Without saying another word, she mounted her horse and urged it forward. It was half a day's ride to the coast, and she wanted to reach it quickly. Her guards rode on either side to offer her the greatest amount of protection.

Efren stood with the appearance of strength as he listened to the horses move farther into the distance. He felt as if he were losing control, if he ever had control in the first place. His kingdom was rapidly declining, and his wife was heading into the eye of the storm. There was nothing he could do now except wait for her return.

Ryshel pushed the thoughts of her children and home away from her mind. If she was to succeed, she would have to be fully dedicated. She would not give in to despair and melancholy as Aubriana had. Ryshel was a strong woman, and she would need all her strength in the days to come.

For hours they rode without halting, until finally they arrived at the coast. A small ship was indeed anchored, awaiting the queen's arrival. The captain, however, did not know her true identity. He was told a noblewoman needed safe passage to Na'zora. The fewer people who knew the truth, the better.

"Good evening," she said to one of the sailors. "I am Rya, and I'll be traveling with you."

The sailor nodded and asked, "Where's your baggage?"

"I won't be needing any," she replied. "Everything I require is waiting for me there."

With a shrug, the sailor led her on board the ship. There were few luxuries to be found. The deck was piled high with crates, and there were only a handful of crewmen aboard.

Leading her below deck, he showed her to a tiny cabin with four cots. "This will be your room," the man said.

Ryshel nodded and hoped she would be the only person to occupy it. Though there were four places to sleep, there was barely enough room to turn around. The presence of three other people would make her feel as if she were suffocating.

The sailor walked away, leaving her in silence. Instead of going to bed, she headed back up to have a look at the stars. The crew was busy shoving off, but she ignored the noise as they called out to one another. Finding a comfortable spot to recline, she gazed up at the night sky. There were no clouds to be seen—only millions of stars and a bright, bluish moon. Closing her eyes, she breathed deeply as the motion of the ship rocked her to sleep. At sunrise she awoke, surprised to find herself still on deck.

"Was your bed not comfortable, Miss?" the ship's captain asked.

"I'm sure it's just fine," she replied.

Though Ryshel had never traveled by sea, she found herself feeling quite at home aboard the small vessel. For days she walked the decks, learning about the immense amount of work that went into sailing. The crew proved to be friendly, and the food was not bad either. The men kept her entertained with stories and song, but when she was alone, thoughts of her family crept back into her mind.

At last the coast of Na'zora came into view, and Ryshel felt her anxiety rise. Waving from the docks was a tall, plain-faced woman, her hair pulled back tightly in a bun. Lady Bartin had received her message.

"Welcome to Na'zora, Lady Rya," she said as Ryshel approached.

"It's nice to meet you," she replied.

"I am Lady Bartin, friend of Princess Aubriana. I received your letter and am most eager to help."

Ryshel smiled in relief. This was the woman who had kept Aubriana informed of Rayne's well-being. "Can you help me get a position in the palace?"

"I can," Lady Bartin replied confidently. "First we'll need to get you some more suitable attire."

Ryshel nodded and climbed inside the waiting carriage. "Who else knows of my arrival?"

"No one," Lady Bartin replied. "I have kept this secret to myself. My husband believes you are a cousin of mine who lives near our southern border. I've made it a point over the past few days to complain about the care Rayne has been receiving. My husband is one of Rayne's appointed guardians, you see."

"That is good to hear," Ryshel said. "That means you might be in need of a new governess for him soon."

"Yes, indeed," she said. "My husband cares little for the rearing of children. I have seven of my own, so he listens to my advice most carefully." She laid a hand on Ryshel's arm and said, "Rayne misses his mother so. Tell me how she is faring."

Looking down at the floor of the carriage, Ryshel replied, "Aubriana is not well. Her heart is broken, and she suffers greatly. That is why I've come."

Lady Bartin sighed. "I feared she would not have the strength for this. We must get you and Rayne back to her as quickly as possible."

That was exactly what Ryshel had in mind. The longer she remained in Na'zora, the greater her chance of making a mistake and being discovered. As soon as an opportunity presented itself, no matter how small, she would attempt to leave with the young prince. Both their lives might depend on it.

Chapter 31

As the sun first peeked over the horizon, Efren awoke to an empty bed. Ryshel was not in his arms, and her warmth was nowhere to be found. *How many days has it been? Is she safe?* Though he was constantly surrounded by servants and advisors, he could not shake the feeling of loneliness his wife's absence had created. Since their marriage, they had never been apart for more than a few hours. He trusted her advice above all others, and he yearned to have her at his side once more.

As he rose from his bed, servants immediately flocked to his side. A bowl of water was held in front of him, allowing him to wash his face. His clothes had been laid out hours ago, and the servants eagerly dressed him for his morning council meeting. But

Efren had no desire to meet with his councilors. Each day they presented him with more bad news, and he simply did not wish to hear it.

It is my duty, he decided with a sigh. How he longed for the days spent in the countryside, when war had yet to consume his kingdom. Gannon had been a strong leader. He had a passion for war that Efren lacked. *In times when war cannot be avoided, perhaps it is better to have a soldier for a king,* he thought. *If only Gannon were here. Even my father would be a better choice than me.*

A servant presented the king with a silver tray, which contained an assortment of breakfast items. Efren waved the servant away. He had no appetite this morning. Followed by his manservant, he walked slowly through the corridor to the council chambers, his footsteps making little sound against the stone floor. His anxiety rose as he approached the door, but he steadied his breathing to hide it. He must stay strong, though given a choice, he would join Aubriana in her melancholy.

Without speaking, Efren entered the council chamber and took his seat at the head of the table. He waited patiently for someone to commence conversation.

"Your Majesty," Duke Arden said, "it pains me to report that Na'zora has now taken the entirety of central Ra'jhou. What is left of our army is now scattered and leaderless. Scouts have reported seeing mages who conjure fire in the northern regions. They are headed our way."

"There is still no word from Pedr or any of the other dwarves?" Efren asked, sitting tall in his seat. *What has become of him?*

"None, Majesty," Arden replied. "Whatever their mission was, it seems they have yet to accomplish it."

"Let us hope they do so before there is no Ra'jhou left to assist." Though he did not show it, Efren was worried the mission had failed. It was possible Pedr had been unsuccessful in persuading the dwarf king, or that he had changed his mind entirely. There was also the possibility that his king had him executed. After all, Efren had sent him back to the person who had banished him. Was he to be another death added to his conscience?

"Majesty," General Willem began, "there are rumors that our missing soldiers have indeed gone into the mountains. Some of the evacuated citizens have knowledge of it."

"I am told many of our smaller forces are fleeing from magefire," Arden added. "They know not how to combat them, so they flee." Looking at Willem, he said, "Not our more experienced forces, of course."

"They are safer among the mountains than they would be here," Efren commented.

"Send out riders, Your Majesty," Willem suggested, ignoring the king's comment. "Your men are loyal and willing to fight. They are scattered, but they have not deserted. They will return if we can locate them."

"Sir, if scouts are reporting that the Na'zoran army is moving this way, then we must make final preparations for a siege," Councilman Faril said. His eyes met the duke's, and he quickly looked away.

Efren leaned his head on his hand as he weighed his options. "We cannot send out riders. They could be lost as well, and we need every man here who can fight when the castle is attacked. Once Na'zora has breached our walls, someone will have to defend the people."

"With all due respect, Your Majesty," Willem began, "we are waiting for an execution. Without the rest of our army, we have almost no protection."

"We have this castle. It is our fortress," the king reminded him.

"Yes, and once their mages burn it to the ground what shall we have?"

"Fire cannot burn stone," Efren replied. "The walls will hold." After a moment, he added, "They have to."

Arden sighed. Though the king was unwilling to try, the duke was still in favor of collecting the missing soldiers. "There may be time to retrieve some of the soldiers before Na'zora reaches us. Perhaps they are gathering in strength and waiting for us to lead them home. I am in favor of sending out riders."

"If they are alive, they should find their way back here on their own," the king said. He would hear no more talk of seeking them out. If they were in the mountains, perhaps they would cut off the Na'zoran troops as they marched on the castle. It would certainly be beneficial to have a group on the outside, as long as Na'zora was unaware of them.

"What preparations remain for the siege?" Arden asked, changing the subject. "The Na'zorans could be here within the month, and there are so many mouths to feed that I cannot say how long we will last." The duke had been incredibly busy overseeing the training of the volunteer soldiers, as well as observing every movement of the traitorous councilors. Luckily, he had employed several young servants who were eager to keep a close eye on the men. All reports had been positive. It seemed the councilors had no further interest in their plot.

"The dwarves are still working on constructing defensive machines. Though some of them are working with wood, which isn't the same as working with stone. I have no idea how well crafted these machines might be, but I suppose they are better than nothing." Willem shook his head, displeased with the castle's lack of defenses. If the king thought walls were all the protection he would need, he was sadly mistaken.

"Food stores are in good supply," Faril reported. Since Ryshel's departure, he had taken over many of her duties among the people at Arden's insistence. With the duke watching his every move, he had been forced to abandon his plan to supplant the king.

"My scouts will continue to monitor Na'zora's progress," Willem stated. "It won't be long now. I'm certain of it."

"Let them come," Efren replied. "They can have my throne instead of the lives of my people if it comes down to that. A throne is nothing to me compared with the well-being of Ra'jhou's citizens."

Arden admired Efren's resolve. He wished he had been privy to the deal Efren had made with the dwarves. It would put his mind at ease if he knew help was on the way. Unfortunately, the king had offered up no information on the subject for fear of a second betrayal.

Chapter 32

Pedr paced impatiently outside the massive stone palace. He and his companions had been waiting hours for the king to decide whether he would meet with them. Finally, a guard came to collect them.

"The king has agreed to give you a few moments of his time," the guard said, motioning the men to follow him.

Inside the palace was a vast, open space. The walls and floor were carved into the cobalt blue stone of the mountain. Large cauldrons lit the way as they pressed on toward the throne room, a journey of nearly a mile. As they reached the door, the guard held up his hand to stop them.

"Pedr is permitted inside. The others must wait here," he said.

The three men exchanged concerned glances. This could only mean trouble. Taking off his backpack, Pedr handed it to Geryl.

"We'll be right here when you've finished," Geryl said, taking the bag.

Pedr nodded and headed through the massive stone doors of the throne room. Inside, the king perched himself high upon an ornately chiseled throne. His queen sat next to him, her throne only slightly lower than the king's. A wide stone ramp led up to them, lined on each side by guards dressed in the finest plate armor. Pedr resisted the urge to roll his eyes. King Oge was obviously enjoying his newfound power and the luxury that came with it.

"I didn't think to see you again," the king said. He sat proudly upon his throne, dressed in his finest satin tunic. Each finger bore a jeweled ring, giving his hands a heavy appearance.

Reaching the king, Pedr bowed low before him. "It is an honor, Your Majesty."

"You were banished from this land," Queen Zella reminded him. "You are lucky we didn't have you killed on sight." Her golden gown nearly swallowed her in its excess of fabric. She wore too much makeup in an effort to appear younger next to her youthful husband, but it gave her skin a thickened appearance instead.

"What urgent business have you brought? Your message mentioned a vast reward?" The king's voice sounded bored but not angry.

"Forgive me for disobeying the order of banishment," Pedr said. "I had no intention of returning to insult your majesties, but I have been offered a proposition from the King of Ra'jhou. He is interested in friendship with our people."

"Our people—" the queen started to say. King Oge held up his hand to silence her.

"Explain quickly," the king said. He had only so much patience, and his wife's objections to Pedr's visit had already used up most of it.

"The kingdom of Ra'jhou has a rather lucrative mine sitting unused near its northern border. I, along with my kinsmen, have begun construction of a settlement there. Unfortunately, the kingdom is at war, and its future is uncertain."

"Let me guess," the king said. "You have come to ask for my help in holding this mine, even if Ra'jhou loses their war. Who is it they are fighting?"

"The kingdom of Na'zora lies south of Ra'jhou. They have skilled mages who are taking over each village and market district. At this very moment, they are marching on Ra'jhou's castle, if they haven't reached it already."

"What does any of this have to do with us?" the queen asked.

"King Efren of Ra'jhou is willing to pay you a stipend from the mine's profits for your assistance."

King Oge laughed. "This king finds himself without allies and too weak to fight. He thinks I'll come to his aid." The king shook his head and laughed again. "A few pieces of ore are not worth my involvement in a war. What's to stop Na'zora and its mages from marching here?"

"The mine—" Pedr began, but was interrupted by the king.

"Don't think I don't see what this is about. You want to control this mine and become wealthy off it. You will have full control, while I sit here waiting for you to send me my fair share."

Pedr had expected this sort of reaction from Oge. He was a young king, still figuring out how he wanted to rule. These words were merely his way of feeling he had the power here, not Pedr. It was time to reveal the information he was withholding. "Your Majesty, this is a silver mine."

King Oge's eyebrows went up as he leaned forward to look at Pedr. "I'm listening," he said.

"You know well that the magical properties of silver are highly prized among our people, as well as among the elves of the isles." Pedr smiled, knowing he had the king's full attention. "You also know that those elves would never have anything to do with a common dwarf such as myself. But a king, they would speak with. A king they will consider worthy of their time. You can arrange a trade that will bring you profits beyond all imagining. I will be nothing more than a humble worker."

King Oge beamed, nearly salivating at the prospect of trade with the elves. Enlightened Elves had ceased dealings with the dwarves on all matters, preferring to deal with humans, who they considered slightly more tolerable. A wealth of silver, with its immense magical properties, would bring them crawling back. The elves had no current supplier of the precious metal, and they had no skill in crafting it. With dwarves added to the equation, and a human king who was most willing to share, there could be no finer deal for the dwarves. All it would require were soldiers, which Oge had in abundance.

"Why doesn't this Ra'jhouan king just sell the silver to the elves outright and cut you out of the equation entirely? What does he need with us?" The queen spoke with contempt, not hiding her dislike for Pedr.

"King Efren needs an ally who is closer to home," Pedr explained. "His men have no idea how to craft the silver to unlock its magical potential, so he needs us dwarves to do that for him." Pedr felt confident he had explained things well enough. How could the king refuse such an offer?

Queen Zella laughed. "Don't you see?" she asked the king. "This is a trick. This king wants your army to save his land, and after you've done your part, he and Pedr will have all the profits. They don't need us at all for this deal with the elves. The elves would rather deal with a human king than a dwarf. We won't be needed once we've delivered the troops."

King Oge nodded, narrowing his eyes. To Pedr, he said, "I have no reason to trust this king. This idea of yours has merit, but how do I know I'll get a cut of the profits?"

"You would be the one negotiating with the elves," Pedr replied. "King Efren would leave everything to you."

Oge shook his head in disbelief. "He wants my army now, and then he expects me to do the negotiating with the elves later. I have no assurance here."

"Your Majesty, I can promise you that King Efren is a man of his word. Why do you dismiss him so readily?" Pedr could not understand why Oge was not eager to take this opportunity. He had plenty of soldiers to spare, and the dwarf-crafted silver would make him the richest king in all Nōl'Deron.

"The fact of the matter is that this king is a blind man who has fought no battles. He hasn't proved himself worthy of my aid." Oge sat back in his seat, his head leaning heavily on his hand.

Pedr reached into his pocket and pulled out a folded piece of parchment. It was time to reveal his final bargaining chip. "I hold in my hand something that will increase the strength of our army, the likes of which have never been seen."

Oge seemed perplexed. "Why has this king not used this for his own army?"

"He does not have the forges nor the proper resources," Pedr explained. "I have brought something from Ra'jhou's mines that, when compounded with an item from our mines, will grant us a weapon like no other. This paper explains the process in the king's own hand."

Oge's eyes gleamed with delight. He was most interested in this new weapon. "Let's have a look, shall we?"

Pedr handed the paper to the king. Oge was a sly man, and not one to be trusted too readily. He had betrayed his own king in order to take his place, and a man such as that would betray anyone to get what he wanted. Pedr would not hand over the missing ingredient, nor the second sheet of parchment, until he had an army ready to march. If Oge was planning to double-cross him, he would never succeed.

Chapter 33

Stepping back to admire his work, Groot felt a sense of pride. The trebuchet had come together nicely in less time than he had anticipated. To his surprise, he saw the king and Duke Arden touring the grounds. He waved his hand to get their attention. The duke noticed him and nodded. After a moment's discussion, the pair were headed to the top of the castle wall to meet with Groot.

Groot bowed slightly before the king. He had little experience in matters of court and wasn't sure what was considered acceptable behavior. Deciding he would talk with the king as he would any other man, he said, "I've built you the finest trebuchet your kingdom has ever seen. She's a beauty to look upon."

Efren ran his hand along the smooth wood of the machine. "What do we have to load into it?" he asked. "How far is its reach?"

"I've had one of your youngsters run out in the field to mark it for me. His legs were longer than mine." He chuckled a bit, and added, "It's got a good reach on it, of that you can be sure. As for what to load, well that's in the works. Some of my men are already gathering rocks for you to use. If all else fails, use the castle when it starts to crumble." He probably should have left out that last bit, but it was too late.

"As a last resort, that isn't a bad idea," Efren commented. "That's assuming when the walls are breached the trebuchet is still functioning."

Arden put a hand up to shield his eyes from the sun and looked into the distance. "I see the white lines your assistant placed to mark the range on this contraption," he said. "You will be erasing that before Na'zora arrives, won't you?"

"Of course," Groot replied, his eyes twinkling. "Don't you worry. I'll have it gone by the end of the day. I just need the men who will be operating it to memorize the spot first. I don't want any shots being wasted."

"Who will be manning the machine?" Arden asked.

"I had a few of your citizens volunteer," Groot said. "One was a little girl. You've got some brave lasses around here, to be sure."

"Indeed we do," Efren agreed.

Groot pointed across the wall, where several female archers stood ready. "Those ladies there are young. I hope they can hit their targets."

"They have been well trained," Arden said. "You'd be surprised." He had overseen their training personally and was quite pleased with what he had seen from them.

Groot offered no argument about their abilities. "They're certainly a brave lot to stand where they are. They're going to be prime targets."

"Do you have any ideas about protecting them?" Arden asked.

"Well, they're behind those walls, so at least they aren't exposed. I'm just afraid that Na'zora will aim hard for that section of the castle once they realize we have archers there."

"Could you reinforce the wall?" Efren asked.

"I'll do my best," Groot replied. "In the meantime, I'll have my men working on special armor for them. It won't stop them from being crushed, but it might help if they're hit by smaller debris."

Efren sighed. "The concept of my castle flying apart disturbs me," he said. "Why is it everyone expects it to fall? Is protection not what a castle is designed for?"

"That's not what I meant, sir," Groot said apologetically. "I've seen battle before, and I know what can happen. I suppose I'm planning for the worst."

"I suppose I'm lucky," the king said.

"In what way, Majesty?" Arden asked.

"I won't have to look upon the faces of the dead when this is over. Whether it is because of my lack of vision or because I am dead myself, I will be spared that horror." His words hung heavily in the air, with Groot and Arden exchanging glances. Neither of them spoke.

Turning to face the archers, Efren said, "These are the bravest among my soldiers. They are average citizens with barely enough training, yet they have volunteered their lives to protect the people of this land. I will not forget what they have done." Efren admired these men and women deeply. If only he could stand next to them in battle, he would feel as if he'd done what he could. Instead, he was expected to sit upon his throne and command what remained of his army. Gannon would not have stood back and waited, but what could Efren do? He had no training in any form of combat.

"Groot, would you teach me how to operate this trebuchet?" Efren asked, to the surprise of both Arden and Groot.

Groot sputtered a moment and said, "Of course I will."

"My manservant will need to know as well in case I am hit. Have armor ready for us both. Nothing fancy. Whatever the other soldiers are wearing will do nicely."

"Majesty, I'd be happy to operate this machine on your behalf," Groot offered. "You're an important man, and you shouldn't put yourself in danger."

Efren shook his head. "This is something I must do."

"Your Majesty, you will be needed elsewhere," Arden protested. "You can't risk your life up here."

"I can and I will," he replied. "Even now, Ryshel is risking her life to save a child. Should I not do the same to save my kingdom and all the souls living within it?"

Arden didn't know what to say. He admired the king's bravery, but he did not agree with his decision.

"You are my First Advisor, and you shall take my place coordinating the army once Na'zora has arrived. The responsibility of distributing goods throughout the siege can fall to whomever you choose."

"As you command, Your Majesty," he replied. There was no point in further argument. The king had spoken, and the duke would obey.

"How soon can you have a second trebuchet built?" Efren asked.

"I can have it in about three days if I focus only on that," the dwarf replied. "I will make it my top priority."

"Who, may I ask, will be manning the second one?" Arden asked.

"Groot may have the honor, if he so chooses," Efren replied.

A broad smile spread across Groot's face. "I'd be delighted."

Chapter 34

With help from Lady Bartin, Ryshel was placed as governess to Prince Rayne. The pair were introduced on her first day in residence, but the boy had not been told her true identity. It would be far too difficult for such a young child to keep a secret.

Ryshel was pleased to see he had been treated well. Except for missing his mother, he was generally happy. His life consisted mostly of play and only a few hours of study each week. Ryshel enjoyed helping him to learn his letters and reading to him at night. He had a bright imagination and a good heart. She longed to tell him the truth about herself, but it was too risky. The sweet young boy probably wouldn't be able to contain his excitement if he knew he might be reunited with his mother.

Though Ryshel wished to leave immediately, there were a few things that she needed to accomplish in order to avoid suspicion. First, she would need to earn the trust of those around her and be seen in the boy's presence by many members of the palace staff. Then, there would be less suspicion if she were seen departing with him. That would take time, but hopefully not too long. Her own children's welfare sat firmly at the back of her mind, and she wondered if she had made the right decision in leaving them behind. She forced herself to believe that they were safe, as long as the castle stood. Efren would do everything in his power to protect them. Ryshel hoped it would be enough.

After a week had passed, Lady Bartin stopped by for a visit. Taking Ryshel aside, she said, "I have arranged for a carriage to meet you this night. It is time for you to go."

Ryshel's heart raced as she nodded her understanding. "I am ready," she said.

That evening, Ryshel dressed herself in a plain dress and concealed herself in a gray hooded cloak. Dismissing all of Rayne's servants, she made sure no one was around to hear the words she was about to say to him.

"Rayne, there is something I need to tell you," she said softly.

Rayne looked up at her, his blue eyes full of cheer as usual.

"My true name is Ryshel. I am your aunt."

Rayne jumped to his feet and bounced up and down. "Auntie Rysh!" he shouted. "Mommy talked about you before she went away."

Ryshel smiled and hugged the boy. "Your mother misses you dearly and has sent me to collect you."

The boy's eyes shone with hope. "I want to be with her more than anything," he said.

"And I shall take you to her," Ryshel promised.

As night fell, she dressed the boy in commoner's clothing and covered him with a large black cloak. She intended to say he was her own son should anyone stop them along the road. With any luck, they would go unnoticed. The carriage was awaiting them only a few yards outside the palace grounds.

The moonless night gave them the best chance they had of not being seen. Quietly, the two left the palace and approached the gates. A single guard stood watch, leaning lazily against the metal bars.

"Who goes there?" he asked as they appeared from the darkness.

"It's only me, the nursemaid Rya," Ryshel replied.

"Who's with you?" the guard asked, looking at the boy. In his commoner clothing, the guard did not suspect his true identity.

"He is my son," she stated.

The guard stared at them a moment longer, but finally he opened the gate. "Go on," he said.

Ryshel's heart skipped a beat as she grabbed Rayne's hand and walked through the gate to freedom. Finally, she could let out the breath she had been holding. They were on their way home at last.

Not a minute after they stepped through the gate, an alarm bell rang out. Someone was aware the prince was missing. Ryshel and Rayne broke into a run as the guard behind them shouted, "Halt!"

Paying the man no heed, they continued to run. Dozens of footsteps sounded behind them on the hard stone path. Ryshel knew she had failed. The guards would overtake her, and she would be separated from the boy as Aubriana had been.

The carriage came into view as the guards closed in on the pair. Her heart fell as the horses sprang into motion. The driver must have heard the alarm and seen the guards. No doubt he wished to avoid putting himself in danger. Ryshel could only stare as her hope rolled away with the carriage.

A strong hand gripped Ryshel's arm and pulled her back. "Where are you going?" he demanded, his breath hot on her face.

Rayne squealed as he was lifted into the air, his hood pushed back from his face. "This is the prince," one of the guards said. "She's tried to kidnap the prince!"

The guard carried the boy back to the castle as Ryshel was dragged along behind. With a firm grip on her arms, they led her down a dark passage to the palace dungeons. The guard flung her into a cell and slammed the door.

"You'll hang for this," he said, spitting on her.

"I am Ryshel, Queen of Ra'jhou, and I demand to be treated with respect!" she declared.

The guard laughed. "Well I'm the King of Whiskey Village, and I demand you buy me a drink." He performed a silly dance to the amusement of the other guards.

"What I have said is true," she replied, crossing her arms. "Take me to your king at once."

The guard laughed again. "My king is away at war. I'll fetch you some paper and you can write him a letter." He grinned at her, revealing blackened teeth.

"Then I demand you take me to whoever is ruling in his stead. I am a queen!"

The guard looked her up and down, wondering if she might be telling the truth. She did not appear intoxicated, and her voice and mannerisms revealed her identity as a noblewoman. "For a price," he said, holding a hand through the bars.

Ryshel stared at the man with hate in her eyes. Reaching into her pocket, she found two small pieces of gold. Placing them in the guard's hand, she said, "Take these. I can give you more once I'm released."

The guard's eyes lit up with delight when he saw the gold. "I'll be back for you in the morning," he said with a grin. "Wouldn't want to wake anyone just yet." With a mock kiss, he added, "Sweet dreams."

The blood rose in Ryshel's face, but she said nothing. Taking a seat on the straw that was strewn on the cold, wet floor, she settled in for the night.

Chapter 35

Aubriana reclined on her bed, her eyes staring blankly at the ceiling. She paid no heed to the knock at her door. A young girl had arrived with a message which contained urgent news from Na'zora.

Ignoring the conversation between her maid and the girl, Aubriana turned to face the balcony. Outside, the Wrathful Mountains stood as proud as ever. *Would that I were absorbed in that stone,* she thought. *Surely a mountain feels no pain.*

Clouds had descended, hiding the tips of the mountains from view. The wind rustled the princess's bed curtains and dried the tears on her face. More tears fell to replace them.

Shala's eyes moved quickly as she read the letter. The information it contained was far too important to keep from the princess. She must be informed. Moving to the bed, Shala stood over her, holding the parchment in her hand. "It's about Queen Ryshel," she said.

Aubriana did not respond. Her eyes remained fixed on the landscape, her ears unhearing.

"My lady," Shala spoke louder. "There is urgent news of Queen Ryshel. She has been taken prisoner."

Those words roused Aubriana, who reached out her hand for the letter. Looking over the words on the page, she began to weep. "Help me dress," she said, her voice raspy. "I must speak to my brother." She crumpled the letter in her hand and pressed it to her chest.

"I could bring the news to the king for you," Shala offered. "You aren't well enough to be out of bed."

Aubriana patted her maid's hand. "This is my duty," she said.

Shala helped the princess to the cushioned bench of her dressing table and went to retrieve an appropriate dress. Returning with a dark green gown, she slipped it over the princess's head. Aubriana stood, allowing the skirt to fall in place. Brushing her hand lightly over the satin, she realized how long it had been since she had dressed. Her days were spent in bed, wearing only a plain cotton chemise.

"This color suits you," Shala said, attempting to make conversation. Too many days had passed in silence. She was happy to see her mistress out of bed for a change. "Have a seat and I'll fix your hair."

Aubriana sat in silence while Shala combed through her messy hair. Though the maid was gentle, there were too many tangles to avoid any pain. Aubriana did not mind. The physical pain took away her numbness and reminded her that she was still alive. Observing herself in the mirror, she realized how pale her face had become. Her eyes seemed distant, lost in the gray that surrounded them. She touched her fingers to the fine lines that had appeared on her forehead. *I was beautiful once,* she thought. *How life has changed me.*

Once Shala had finished with her, she said, "You look like a princess again."

Aubriana managed a weak smile, though she no longer felt like a princess. Someone else, it seemed, now inhabited the shell the princess had left behind.

"Let me come with you," Shala requested. The princess was not strong enough to walk so far on her own. Her legs were wobbly, her steps uncertain.

With a nod, Aubriana took her maid's arm. Together they began the slow march to the throne room, where Efren was holding court. Aubriana clutched the letter tightly in her hand and tried to steady her breathing. There was no choice—she must face the king. This news was too important to keep from him, no matter how he might react.

Two guards stood at attention outside the door. Their faces displayed surprise at seeing the princess. To their knowledge, she had not left her bedchamber for weeks.

"I need to see the king," she said in a low voice. "It is a matter of urgency."

The guards looked at each other before opening the door. The king's page stood on the other side.

"What is it?" he asked.

"Princess Aubriana requests an audience with His Majesty," the guard said. "She says it is urgent."

The page nodded and motioned for Aubriana to enter. In a loud voice, he announced her presence.

Aubriana approached the king, still supported by her maid. With the best curtsy her weakened legs could manage, she said, "My Brother King, I come bearing news. A dear friend of mine in Na'zora has sent word of Ryshel."

Efren sat forward in his seat. "Tell me," he said. "Did she arrive safely? Is she on her way home?"

Aubriana swallowed hard and closed her eyes. "She did arrive safely and was given a position as governess to Rayne." Her voice shook as she added, "A few days ago, she was taken prisoner while trying to escape with him."

Efren was stunned by the news. He sat motionless, absorbing the words his sister had spoken. Closing his eyes, he asked, "What will they do with her? Will she be executed?"

"Her insistence that she is a queen has fallen on deaf ears. She is currently housed in the dungeons." Aubriana looked down at her feet, her head feeling too heavy to lift. This was her own fault. Ryshel should never have gone. If Aubriana had not been so distraught, Ryshel would never have felt compelled to attempt something so dangerous. It was Aubriana's own betrayal that had led to this. She had cost Efren everything—his kingdom and the woman he loved. "Forgive me," she whispered.

Laying his head in his hands, Efren wept. This news was more difficult to bear than the impending loss of his kingdom. Even in his worst imaginings, he had always been killed before his wife and children. Now he might have to live with the reality that she was never coming home. His beloved was suffering and would surely be killed. There was nothing he could do to save her.

Aubriana gathered herself and approached the throne. Taking her brother's hands in hers, she said, "Have hope, my king. My friends will do everything they can to free her. They believe it's only a matter of gold."

Efren paid no heed to her words.

Chapter 36

Ryshel sat wedged in the corner of her prison cell, nibbling on a small crust of bread. At first she had refused the food brought to her, insisting she should be given a proper meal. The guard would only shrug and stuff the food into his own mouth while she watched. After two days without eating, she decided it was better to take what she was given. If there were any chance she would be brought before the king to plead her case, she did not plan to do so weary from hunger. She took each meal, no matter how meager, without a word.

There were no visible windows, so she relied on the guards to give her an accurate account of the passage of time. With only pale torchlight available to her eyes, she could not tell the difference between night and day. Still, the darkness shielded her from some of the horrors of her prison. Screams echoed off the walls, but she could not see the face of the sufferer, nor could she see his blood pooling red on the stone floor. The squeaking of rodents also filled her ears, but she could not see their tiny eyes shining in the darkness.

Despite her pitiful conditions, the guards had not treated her too badly. For the most part, she held her tongue, not wanting to antagonize them and worsen the situation. They left her alone, forgetting about her claims of royalty. She could only hope that Lady Bartin was working to find a solution to her imprisonment. There was nothing to do but wait.

Did Efren know of her predicament? She hoped he did not. He already had so much on his mind, and the safety of the kingdom rested on his shoulders. Ryshel did not wish to add yet another burden to her troubled husband.

Though she listened closely to the conversations between the guards, she heard no word of the war with Ra'jhou. Any news would be welcome. Not knowing if the castle still stood was driving her mad. While she sat idle in the darkness, her children could be in serious danger.

Why did I come here? she wondered. *Would it not have been better to remain in Ra'jhou and await the outcome of the war? Even if we had lost, at least I would have died alongside my loved ones, not alone in a foreign land.*

Ryshel cursed her own stubbornness. Rayne was in no danger here, that much was certain. He was Tyrol's only heir, and he would naturally be protected. Shaking the thoughts away, she determined it was best to stick by her decision rather than give in to despair. Aubriana deserved to have her child at her side. Ryshel had erred in the manner of escaping, and her capture was her own fault. If she had planned a better escape, she would be back in Ra'jhou by now, with the young prince at her side.

Another thought occurred to her that filled her with dread. Had Lady Bartin's part in this scheme been discovered? Was she under arrest as well? If so, there was no one left to help her. None of Aubriana's friends would want to be involved after this. They would face the king's wrath, just as Ryshel herself would. What would his punishment be?

Footsteps sounded through the darkness, making their way closer and closer to her cell. Ryshel rose to her feet and peered into the distance. She stepped back, startled as a guard appeared. She had not realized he was so close by.

"Some water, miss," he said, thrusting a wooden cup between the bars.

Aubriana could see the youthfulness of his face. Taking the cup, she said, "Thank you for your kindness."

He nodded and said, "It's not right to keep a lady down here."

With a half-smile, she replied, "I quite agree with you."

The guard's expression seemed puzzled. "You don't talk like an ordinary prisoner. If you don't mind my asking, what was your crime?"

"Attempting to kidnap the prince, or so they say," she replied, handing the cup back to him.

"You're the one who caused all that commotion the other night?" His mouth hung open as he tried to comprehend her crime. "I never heard it was a woman they caught."

"Indeed it was," she responded. "I've been here ever since."

"Still, it isn't right to keep a woman here," he stated. "This place isn't fit for any woman, even a criminal." He turned and headed back into the darkness.

Aubriana listened to his footsteps as he disappeared from sight. She was grateful for the company, if only for a brief moment. Resigning herself to the silence once more, she retreated back to the corner of her cell and leaned her back against the wall.

Hours or possibly days passed before she heard footsteps approaching her cell once more. The young guard had returned to bring her something to eat. He said nothing, but a concerned frown graced his features as the dim light of his torch fell upon Ryshel's face. Through the bars, he handed her a small bundle before heading back into the darkness.

Untying the cloth, Ryshel smiled at what she saw inside: a small wedge of cheese, a slice of warm bread, and a handful of raisins. This food was far too good for a prisoner. The guard had given her his own meal.

"Thank you," she said to the darkness, hoping the young man would hear. His compassion brought tears to her eyes. Even here in the most horrible place she could imagine, there was kindness and humanity. Perhaps there was hope for her after all.

When next the guard returned, she was determined to tell him who she was. If she could convince him of her true identity, she might have a chance at an audience with King Tyrol. She doubted he would grant her freedom, but he might at least give her better accommodations. Even a swift execution would be better than lingering in this place. Ryshel finished her meal, hoping the guard would return soon.

Chapter 37

"Scouts are reporting the Na'zorans are closing in, Your Majesty. They will be here within a few days." Duke Arden stood firm as he delivered the grim news. Ra'jhou's final stand was about to commence.

"How are the preparations going?" Efren asked. "Do we have enough food for everyone?"

"We have collected all the supplies that could be found and stored them within the castle. With rationing, we should last at least a month."

"What of our army?" the king asked.

"General Willem has briefed the soldiers we have remaining, and they are prepared to do battle."

"We should take the time to arm the citizens as well," Efren said. "If the walls are breached, they might have to defend themselves. I would have them prepared for it."

"Very well, Your Majesty."

"Groot can assist you," Efren added. "He and his crew should have enough items to supply those who want them."

With a bow, Arden exited the throne room to seek out the dwarf craftsman. The activity in the courtyard was minimal, and there were no signs that the citizens were panicking. There had been enough time to prepare, and it seemed there was no last-minute rush. Arden was glad to see that the people seemed at ease. Beneath their brave exteriors, he was sure they were as frightened as he was. A decisive battle was about to begin, and Ra'jhou's survival was at stake. He could not help admiring the resolve of the people.

Groot was perched upon the castle wall next to the second trebuchet he had constructed. Noticing Arden's arrival, Groot said, "I keep checking the horizon for soldiers. I haven't seen any yet."

"They'll be here soon enough," Arden replied. "King Efren wants the citizens armed. Can you see to it?"

"Aye," the dwarf replied. His workers had retrieved all unused armor pieces and weapons that had been stored in the castle over the past few generations. Only a small number of pieces had been damaged beyond repair. Groot's men had repaired the rest as best they could. They wouldn't last long in a fight, but they were far better than nothing.

Arden headed off to announce the need for more volunteers. He visited each camp, instructing them to meet with the dwarves if they would like to obtain a weapon. Many citizens were already barricaded inside the castle, and he did not offer to arm them. These were the citizens who would need to flee if the battle went ill. They were either too old or too young, and the rest were women who were needed to look after the children and provide medical attention should any of them become injured. The only information Arden could give them was to make them aware of the correct route to take should they need to flee into the mountains. It would be a last resort, but it might be necessary if the castle fell. There was no way of knowing whether the Na'zorans would spare their lives.

Groot gathered his men and helped them place the armor and weapons into carts. By the time they had finished, long lines of citizens had formed. Nearly every man, including boys as young as ten years of age, along with a large portion of women, waited for the dwarves to deliver the weapons.

Handing a dagger to a woman clutching a baby, Groot said, "Shouldn't you be down in the cellars? It would be safer for your baby."

The woman glared at him, making him wish he'd kept his opinion to himself. "If I have to kill to defend my child, I will do it gladly," she stated. Taking the dagger, she marched away in a huff.

Groot shook his head. Perhaps dwarf women would do the same if faced with a hopeless situation. In the future, he would hold his tongue before the women of Ra'jhou. They were clearly made of stronger stuff than he had anticipated.

A cheer broke out among the people, causing Groot to look up from his work. To his surprise, he saw King Efren making his way through the crowds. His manservant was not far behind, directing the king toward the dwarf.

"Your Majesty," Groot said as the king approached. "My kinsmen and I have been busy arming your people this morning. They aren't the best trained soldiers, but they'll do. They certainly have spirit."

"You completed the second trebuchet, I'm told," Efren said.

"I have," Groot replied. "I'll take you to it if you like."

The king nodded and followed Groot to the top of the castle wall where the second trebuchet stood. Efren clutched at the wood to test its strength.

"It seems sturdy enough," he commented.

"My finest work," Groot responded, his eyes gleaming.

"I am grateful for the assistance you and your people have provided me," Efren said. "Have you had any word from Pedr or the dwarves who left with him?" With no news of the dwarf, Efren had begun to wonder whether his trust had been misplaced. After all, he had known the dwarf only a few minutes before sending him off on a mission of grave importance. His number of mistakes seemed to be mounting, and his mind was occupied by regrets.

"None at all, Majesty," he admitted. Though he wasn't fully aware of Pedr's mission, he knew it was dangerous to send him to speak with King Oge. Pedr had been banished, and it was unlikely the king would be happy to receive him.

"I have placed a great deal of trust in Pedr," Efren stated. "You know him better than I do. Is there any chance he might return with an army of his own? He knows our situation is dire, and we would not be difficult to defeat. He is aware of all our defenses. I worry I've placed my trust in him too easily."

Groot replied, "Your Majesty, Pedr is the most loyal man I've ever known. If he made you a promise, he'll do whatever he can to keep it. You have my word on that." There was no doubt in his mind that Pedr would remain loyal to King Efren.

Efren nodded. "Pedr may be honorable, but what of King Oge? He might see an opportunity that he cannot pass up. This kingdom is vulnerable from too many sides."

Groot did not know what to say. King Oge had come to the throne through questionable means, and it would not be a far reach for him to invade a troubled kingdom, especially if there were riches to be found. Not wanting to burden the king further, Groot kept this information to himself.

Chapter 38

Three days later, the Na'zorans descended on the castle. King Tyrol rode at the front, leading his armies with pride. In total, his craftsmen had managed to build six working catapults and a ram. There were no towers to help scale the walls of the castle fortress. The scarcity of resources and the king's impatience had forced them to travel before a single tower could be completed.

Tyrol observed as four catapults were moved into position by horses, led by the skilled hands of his engineers. The other two catapults, however, were moved by soldiers. There had not been enough horses to supply his cavalry and pull all of the siege equipment. The soldiers who pushed the catapult were quickly becoming exhausted. A few had been injured en route and had to be sent away.

"How close would you like us to get today?" Lieutenant Jak asked. "I recommend caution. We can't be sure what weapons the Ra'jhouans might have."

Tyrol laughed and said, "If they had defensive weapons, they would have used them to halt our advance." After a moment of thought, he added, "But I don't want to be too close to them for now. Let them quake with fear at our approach. Perhaps the blind man will be so frightened he will offer me his throne without a fight."

"He could have done that already, Your Majesty," Lieutenant Jak pointed out.

Tyrol gave him a scathing look. "He's obviously a proud man," he said. "We will wait a while before firing the catapults. I don't want my new castle too damaged. Repairs will be costly. Be sure the mages hold their fire for now as well."

"Of course, Majesty," Jak replied. "Siege warfare makes men idle. What task shall I put the men to while we wait?"

"Have them build shield walls between us and the castle. I'm sure they've rounded up a few archers to hide behind those walls. I wouldn't want anyone to be hit."

* * * * *

From his throne room, Efren could hear the sounds of the approaching army. Their feet marched in time, their steps echoing in his ears. Horses whinnied in the distance, and hammers rang out as the invaders prepared their camps. With only a month of food stored away to feed the entire castle, the Na'zorans wouldn't have to wait long for their victory.

"Duke Arden," Efren began, "escort me to the walls. I would greet this army that has come to conquer us."

Without a word, Arden reached for the king's arm. Was the king ready to surrender? Doing so could potentially save many lives, but Tyrol could not be trusted. He may well annihilate the citizens of Ra'jhou, intending to fill the kingdom with his own people. Perhaps he would divide it into large portions for his noble supporters. The massive funds required to train and outfit his mages must have come from somewhere, and Arden suspected Tyrol would owe favors to many wealthy people.

The sun shone brightly in the sky as the pair ascended the castle walls. Groot was positioned at his trebuchet, watching the crowd gather below. He bowed before the king as he came into view and followed behind him in case there were orders he needed to hear.

Efren stood upon the wall facing the invading army. Though he could not see them, he could feel their presence and sense their malice. The sound of their axes chopping at trees that had stood a hundred years filled his ears. Smoke from their fires filled his nostrils. The landscape of Ra'jhou might never be the same again.

"Are they building a wall?" Efren asked.

"They are, Your Majesty," Arden replied. "They likely wish to protect themselves from our arrows."

"Their walls won't hold up to Groot's trebuchets. Are they in range?"

"Not yet," Groot responded. "The wall they're building will be too close for the trebuchet to hit, and their troops are too far back." Pausing, he added, "For now."

Efren nodded. "When they've constructed the wall, burn it."

Groot grinned and looked at Duke Arden, who was obviously puzzled. "King Efren had me deliver an oily concoction and cotton strips to our archers. They can shoot fire arrows."

Duke Arden raised his eyebrows approvingly.

"Their supplies won't last long, I'm afraid, but destroying their wall will at least dishearten our enemy," Efren stated.

Groot said, "The king's being conservative in his estimate. That chemical of his burns hotter than anything I've ever seen. It won't use up the arrows too quickly."

Once again Arden was confused. Apparently, he had not been privy to all the king's preparations for war. "What chemical would that be?" he asked.

"It's something I've been dabbling with for a while," Efren explained. "It won't get us far, but it will help for a while." Turning away from the army, he said, "I think it's time I was outfitted for battle. I intend to be on this wall when the invaders move into range."

Arden sighed quietly. It would seem Efren still intended to man the trebuchet himself. Perhaps he hoped to be killed in battle, rather than awaiting an execution at Tyrol's hands. If the king was determined to die for his kingdom, Arden would give him his full support. "Your Majesty, I would like to volunteer to aim the contraption for you." If this was truly the end, Arden wouldn't need to continue his duties around the castle. Knowing he would make a poor foot soldier, he decided it was better to join the king upon the walls. Dying at the king's side would be an honor.

Efren smiled and placed his hand on the duke's back. "I welcome your assistance."

Taking their leave, the two went back inside to don their armor. Groot watched them with admiration as they walked away. Arden was not a battle-seasoned veteran. That was plain to see. He had spent his life in refined luxury, not training with a sword. His willingness to join in the fighting was commendable. Efren's dedication was worthy of song. Had he been born a dwarf, he would have been discarded. Groot could not imagine a braver or more loving sovereign. If they survived this onslaught, Groot would be honored to serve this king for the remainder of his life.

Chapter 39

It took days to convince King Oge to ally with Ra'jhou. He had demanded a demonstration of Efren's invention before he would consider the prospect of an alliance. Luckily, Efren's instructions were clear and precise, giving the dwarven craftsmen everything they needed to construct the invaluable weapons. The king was so impressed, he ordered his generals to make ready at once.

After a few days preparation, the army began to march. Among their supplies were the new weapons that would give the dwarves an advantage against Na'zora. Efren had studied many long hours to perfect their construction, and he had told no one except Pedr. Even the servants who had assisted the king in his studies were unaware of the invention. Efren had made sure not to let the same servant assist him too long, for fear they might uncover his plan.

Under cover of night, Pedr journeyed down the mountain, accompanied by an army of dwarves. Though they moved in darkness, their steps were far from quiet. Their heavy footfalls echoed through the night, frightening the nocturnal creatures in their path.

"It's a good thing we don't need to rely on secrecy," Geryl joked.

"When the dwarves are marching, everyone knows it," Pedr replied with a laugh.

"Are you ever going to tell me what you and the king talked about?" Geryl asked. He had been kept in the dark about the whole situation, even though he had stayed faithfully at Pedr's side throughout the journey.

"Which king? Oge?"

"Either one, really," Geryl responded. "You spent a lot of time talking with both of them."

Pedr grinned, his teeth glistening in the darkness. "You'll find out soon enough," he said. "Besides, most of the soldiers here already know. Maybe you can pry it out of one of them."

"I already tried," he admitted. "None of them will say a word. Apparently it's a secret."

"Apparently," Pedr echoed. Slapping his friend on the back, he added, "Trust me, it's worth the wait."

Geryl shook his head, still wishing he knew the full story. Pedr had made a bargain with two kings, and he wondered how it might affect him and the new settlement near Ra'jhou. The two men had been friends for many years, so he trusted that whatever the secret was, it had their families' best interests at heart.

Bor, whose eyes were younger than those of his companions, walked ahead of Pedr and Geryl as a scout. As he proceeded down the mountainside, he caught sight of a campfire just ahead. He rushed back to let the others know there might be trouble ahead.

Hurrying toward one of the generals, Bor said, "There's a campfire ahead. It could be enemies."

Immediately, the general ordered the dwarves to halt their descent and prepare to attack.

Pedr strode forward to look for himself. "I don't think those are Na'zorans," Pedr informed the general. "I doubt they'd be at this height in the mountains. That wouldn't be the quickest route to the castle. I'd bet these are Ra'jhouans."

"Why would they be hiding in the mountains?" the general asked.

"They're scattered," Pedr replied. "Hundreds of citizens have been displaced. There might even be guards or soldiers among them."

"I'll send someone in to find out," the general stated. "The rest of us will remain hidden and ready to attack."

Pedr shook his head. He was certain these people were not a threat. If this was an invading army, they wouldn't give their position away so easily by lighting a campfire. "I'll go in and have a look," Pedr volunteered.

"Suit yourself," the general replied. "If you aren't back in twenty minutes, we'll move in."

Pedr hurried down the mountain to the camp. Sure enough, unarmed citizens were gathered close to the fire, trying to stay warm in the chilly mountain air.

"Hello there," Pedr said, announcing his presence. He held up both hands so the men and women could see he wasn't armed.

"Greetings," a tall, bearded man said. "What brings you here?"

"I'm here to help," he explained. "You are Ra'jhouans, I take it?"

"We are indeed," the man replied. "Our village was destroyed weeks ago, and our path to the castle was cut off by the Na'zoran army. We've set up camp here to await the end of the war."

"Are there soldiers among you?" Pedr asked.

"Not in this camp," he replied. "There is a good portion of our army a bit farther north. They've been looking for a safe route back to the castle, but so far they've failed to find one. There aren't enough of them to break the enemy line."

Pedr grinned. "There will be now." He whistled to his companions and waved his hands, urging them to come forward.

From the darkness, hundreds of dwarf soldiers appeared. The gathered Ra'jhouans cheered at the sight.

"You've come to save us all!" the bearded man shouted.

"Well, there's still the small matter of Na'zora's mages, and let's not forget we're still outnumbered," Pedr pointed out. "We'll do our best, though."

The bearded man nodded. "I'll lead you to the soldiers' camp," he said, grabbing a torch from the fire.

They walked until dawn before they reached the gathered Ra'jhouan soldiers. There were only about three hundred of them that Pedr could see, but even a few were better than none. The soldiers were happy to see the dwarves, who had brought a few extra weapons to share. Hope filled the men as they beheld the sight of their reinforcements.

The man introduced Pedr to the lieutenant who was in charge of the scattered army. "It's good to have you on our side," the lieutenant said, shaking Pedr's hand. "We've kept a close eye on the situation, and Na'zora is already in position at the castle. They have not yet begun their attack, but they will soon."

"Let's hope we're able to break the siege, then," Pedr replied.

As light filled the sky, the men were eager to march. The scouts had reported no further movement by the Na'zorans, but the situation could change at any moment.

"Do we march for the castle in full force?" Pedr asked.

"No," the dwarf general responded. "There's been a change in plans."

Chapter 40

Thunder crashed against the walls of the castle, its voice booming throughout the stone corridors. Cries from women and children rang through the air as the frightened citizens barricaded themselves inside. Soldiers stationed on the walls took cover, fearing the castle might come apart at the seams.

A roar erupted from the invading army as they moved themselves into battle formation. The ground shook beneath their feet as they marched, and the air swirled hot around the mages as they began to conjure their flames.

Efren sat motionless upon his throne, the thunder echoing in his hears. He swallowed hard and steadied his breathing. His face showed no sign of emotion.

"Your Majesty, Na'zora is attacking," Arden announced. "They are in formation outside our walls."

Another crash of thunder reverberated through the castle, followed quickly by a second and a third. The assembled nobles at court looked nervously at one another, wondering if they should take refuge in the lower levels.

"Is that sound coming from the mages?" Councilman Faril asked. "Are they taking down the castle?"

"It could only be," Arden replied.

Efren shook his head, a spark of hope showing on his face. "That is not magefire," he said with confidence. "That is our salvation." He rose to his feet, extending a hand to his First Advisor.

Reaching for the king's arm, Arden gripped it firmly. They exited the throne room together, followed by the entire council and assembled nobles. Arden had no idea of the king's destination. Instead, he allowed the king to lead him as their footsteps echoed through the corridor. Finally, Efren halted near a thin, rectangular window.

"Duke Arden, could you tell me what you see outside this window?"

Arden peered outside, first looking down into the courtyard. The area had been evacuated. "I see nothing, Your Majesty," he said. "There are no soldiers or citizens present in the courtyard."

Urgency rose in the king's voice. "Beyond that. What do you see?"

Arden focused his gaze on the area beyond the castle courtyard, where the Na'zoran army was gathered. "I see legions of Na'zoran soldiers," he said, his eyes drinking in the scene. Wrinkling his brow, he added, "They're all facing away from the castle."

"What else do you see?" Efren asked. "Look beyond the Na'zorans."

In the distance, Arden's eyes fell upon an army of dwarves. His heart nearly stopped as he realized they were attacking the Na'zorans. "There are dwarves!" Arden shouted. "They've come to help us!"

The nobles who had gathered behind the king began chattering over one another. Straining their necks and shoving each other out of the way, they struggled to catch a glimpse of the spectacle outside. Another boom thundered through the castle, and the crowd fell silent.

"What is that sound? Are the mages winning? Do the dwarves still stand?" Councilman Faril asked anxiously.

"I cannot see," Arden replied, "but surely it is the mages firing at the dwarves."

"No, it is not the mages," Efren stated. "It is our friends the dwarves who are wielding this fire. They have alloy vessels full of powder that explode upon impact. It is a technology previously unknown to us. Through many long hours of study and experimentation, I discovered the correct formula and the safest method of transporting it."

Arden stared open-mouthed at the king, unable to believe his ears. King Efren had invented a weapon capable of taking out Na'zora's army. His creation had saved what was left of his kingdom and all the lives barricaded inside the castle. "You invented this? Why did you need the dwarves? Why did you not arm our own soldiers with this?"

"We do not have the resources necessary to craft the vessels," the king explained. "Nor do we have the proper ingredients to put inside them. The dwarves have all but one necessary element available in abundance. The other is found here, beneath this castle."

The councilors could not contain their excitement as they erupted into applause, cheering the king in his victory. "All hail King Efren!" they cried in unison.

General Willem burst through the castle doors, running at top speed up the steps toward the throne room. Finding the entire court assembled in the hallway, he stopped short. "Majesty, the dwarves have attacked Na'zora! Their army is surrounded, their mages destroyed by fire!"

Efren only smiled in response, his gaze still turned to the window. The sunlight beamed upon his face, and he welcomed its warmth.

Arden stated, "We're already aware, General Willem. King Efren has arranged it all."

"Then he has done what my army could not," Willem admitted.

"You have done what you could under the circumstances," Efren said, placing his hand on the general's shoulder. "Your leadership and council have served this kingdom well. I could not wish for a better general to command my army."

Willem felt humbled by the king's praise. "I have disagreed with you and accused you of weakness," he admitted. "I will never doubt you again."

Efren nodded. He held no animosity toward the general who had spoken out against him at times. It was true that Efren had no experience when it came to war. He was grateful to have an experienced general to lead his armies. Gannon had placed his trust in this man, and Efren would as well.

"The Na'zorans will not last long against those dwarves and their firebombs," Arden said, still staring out the window. A broad smile crept across his face as he watched Na'zoran soldiers fleeing the flames. Whatever was in those vessels created bright red flames, the very sight of which sent a chill down the spines of the enemy.

"Majesty, these dwarves have also found the men who were missing from our own army," Willem said. "It seems they ran into each other in the mountains."

"That is fantastic news as well," Efren replied.

"Your Majesty, may I employ these dwarves to take back our conquered lands?" Willem asked.

"Permission granted," Efren responded.

As Willem turned to leave, Arden continued observing from the window. "The Na'zorans have thrown down their weapons," he announced. "They've given up!"

"Take me back to my throne," Efren told him. "I am expecting a visit from a king."

"Gladly," Arden said, taking the king's arm.

Chapter 41

King Tyrol watched in horror as his mages were struck down by the dwarves. The soldiers assigned to guard them fled in terror as the fires raged all around them. There had been no time for the mages to complete their spells—not one of them had managed to throw a single fireball. Tyrol's prized mages were no more.

Lieutenant Jak rushed to the king's side, "Your Majesty, we are beset on all sides!"

Another explosion rocked the ground, sending flames in Tyrol's direction. In a panic, his horse reared, throwing him roughly to the ground. Though uninjured, the event only furthered the king's rage. "Pull our men back!" he shouted to the lieutenant.

The king rose to his feet, brushing the dust away from his armor. Where had he gone wrong? This was supposed to be his moment of glory. As he looked around, he saw nothing but the destruction of his own troops.

The Na'zoran army attempted to rally to its king. The men trod carefully, avoiding the many fires that were burning upon the ground. Each of the catapults they had constructed were now engulfed in flames, and the wall that was intended to protect them from archers had been obliterated.

Though there were few horses left on the scene, Tyrol spotted a single rider making his way through the chaos. "Your Majesty!" the rider cried as he approached. Spotting the king amid the crowd, the man dismounted and bowed. "I narrowly escaped an attack early this morning. I was the only survivor."

"What attack?" the king asked. "Where?"

"I was stationed many miles to the south," the man explained. "We were stockpiling supplies for the siege. The dwarves arrived this morning, Your Majesty. They destroyed everything! I was lucky to escape with my life."

Tyrol spat on the ground as he listened to the news. A second unit of dwarf soldiers was moving south, taking back the lands he had conquered. "How many men were there?" he asked.

"It was chaos with the explosions," the man replied. "I could not say."

Tyrol worried there might be enough dwarves to invade his own kingdom. What was to stop them? With the entirety of his army here and his mages dead, there was no one left to defend Na'zora. In his desire to possess the kingdom to his north, he may have lost everything.

"Find me a horse!" he cried. "We must retreat!" His eyes scanned the field, but the few horses he spotted were too far away, running frantically from the scene. The messenger's horse was plainly exhausted from its long journey, and it would not be able carry the king far enough away.

"Majesty," Lieutenant Jak said. "There is no hope of retreat. The dwarves are too many, and they stand between us and any hope of escape. There is nowhere to go."

"You would have me surrender?" he asked, his face red with anger.

Jak looked at the ground, not wanting to say the words that needed to be said. The siege was over. There was no chance of taking Ra'jhou, and there was no place to run. They would have to face the wrath of their enemies.

Tyrol closed his eyes to block out the scene in front of him. "Tell all of our men to cease fighting. Find the commander of the dwarves and tell him we are beaten." The words tasted bitter in his mouth as he said them, his voice thick and low. Never in his wildest imaginings had this occurred. Ra'jhou was a pitiful kingdom led by a blind man. It had no allies and barely any army. How could he have failed?

"Lay down your weapons!" Jak called as he made his way through the ranks. The cry echoed through the field as the Na'zorans accepted their defeat.

One of the dwarf generals took notice of the Na'zoran surrender and ordered his men to cease firing. He stood proudly, waiting for the king to address him. Instead, it was Jak who came forward.

"Na'zora surrenders," the lieutenant said, holding his head high. Though his army was defeated, he would not stand ashamed. He had served his king well, and he would not grovel before this dwarf.

"Only your king can surrender," the dwarf said. "When I hear those words from his lips, I'll accept it. Until then, my armies continue to march. Let him know we won't be stopping at the border, so he'd better make it quick. A good portion of our forces headed out for Na'zora at dawn. If he waits until nightfall, I won't dispatch a messenger telling them to halt." With a grin, the dwarf crossed his arms and added, "You'd best see to your king."

Slowly, Jak turned and began the march back to King Tyrol's position. "Majesty," he began, "the dwarf would like to hear you surrender personally. If you refuse, he says his army will invade Na'zora."

Tyrol scowled, a low rumble sounding from his throat. "I will kill this dwarf," he stated, his hand moving to the hilt of his sword.

"Your Majesty, they will kill you!" Jak replied. "You mustn't try something so foolish."

Tyrol's eyes flashed with hatred, but he knew Jak's words contained wisdom. If he attacked the dwarf general, the rest of the dwarf army would kill him. History would remember him as a fool who had thrown his life away. No, he would not allow that to happen. He must survive and continue to lead Na'zora. Perhaps he would take revenge on the dwarves another day.

Summoning his pride, the defeated king marched forward to face the general. "My army surrenders," he stated, his voice bold and clear.

The dwarf smirked. "I accept your surrender, and I have a message for you." The general turned and motioned Pedr to his side.

Hurrying to his side, Pedr presented a piece of parchment to King Tyrol. Snatching the letter from the dwarf's hand, Tyrol eyed him suspiciously.

"What is this?" he demanded.

"A letter from King Efren," Pedr replied. "I suggest you take him up on his offer."

Scowling, Tyrol unfolded the parchment and read these words:

Most Honorable King Tyrol,

I, Efren, King of Ra'jhou, invite you to a conference within my castle. It seems you have run into some friends of mine who would be all too delighted to watch you burn. They have an affinity for fire, just as your mages once did. There are matters I would discuss with you. I await your arrival.

Looking up from the parchment, Tyrol found himself closely surrounded by dwarves. To his dismay, they grabbed his arms and dragged him toward the castle.

"This is outrageous!" he shouted. "I am a king!"

The dwarves only laughed.

Chapter 42

Duke Arden could barely contain the amusement in his voice as he announced the arrival of King Tyrol. "Your Majesty, King Tyrol has come to meet with you."

Still being half-dragged by the dwarves, Tyrol entered the throne room. A look of disgust graced his visage as the dwarves released their grip. Straightening the front of his tunic, he stuck out his chest and lifted his head high.

"It is customary to bow before a king," Arden stated proudly.

Tyrol refused, maintaining his defiant stance. Glancing at each other, the dwarves grabbed hold of him once more, forcing him to his knees. With a nod from Arden, they backed away, allowing Tyrol to his feet once more.

"Welcome, King Tyrol," Efren said, sitting upon his throne. "Your arrival has come at a great price."

Tyrol said nothing. Though he had many words to say, none of them would help his situation. This meeting was a formality that would be over quickly. Once he was back in Na'zora, he could forget any promise he made here. His historians would write what he commanded, and it would not include the demands of a blind man pretending to be a king.

"Your surrender brings an end to this war," Efren stated. "I look forward to a future of peace."

"I would expect better treatment, but these friends of yours from the mountains have no respect for kings." Tyrol's voice was full of contempt. If he had any idea Ra'jhou had such an ally, he never would have attempted the siege. The fire weapons wielded by the dwarves were more powerful than any magefire. Given a chance to prepare, Tyrol felt certain he would have found a way to combat them.

"These friends of mine would respect you more had you earned it," Efren replied. "Your friends upon the sea, on the other hand, found you quite worthy of respect. It took much effort to convince them otherwise."

"It was you who convinced the Enlightened Elves to withdraw their aid," Tyrol said, realizing what had happened.

Master Uhnar had provided Efren with the names of several members of the Grand Council on the Sunswept Isles. Efren had written each of them numerous times until he finally convinced them to withdraw. The money paid them by King Tyrol was a vast sum, but it could not compare with dwarf-crafted silver, which Efren promised in hopes that he would eventually win dwarven support. The offer had proved too difficult to resist for the Enlightened Elves, who prized this metal above all others. With a steady supply from Ra'jhou's mine, they would use the precious silver to craft items of unimaginable power. With the elves out of the equation, Na'zora was left without a potion supplier. Had the war continued, Na'zora's mages would have proved useless within a matter of days.

"Indeed, it was I who convinced them to cease their shipments to you, and now I have some demands of my own," Efren replied. "You are holding my wife and my nephew. I want them returned immediately. My army is marching south to reclaim our conquered cities. They will continue into Na'zora until they reach your palace. That is, unless my wife is returned before then."

"I heard a rumor that a queen was in my dungeons," he said. "I did not believe it. I will see that your wife is released at once and escorted to the border. She has not been harmed, as far as I know."

"I will hold you to that," Efren said. "If she is harmed in any way, you will see retaliation on a level you could never imagine." His face reflected the sincerity behind his threat. "I also expect your kingdom to make amends. You have destroyed many of my cities in your path, and you will help to rebuild them."

Not wanting to admit that his kingdom was low on funds, King Tyrol simply agreed. "I will," he stated flatly. Tyrol was convinced he could easily back out of such an agreement once he returned to his own kingdom.

"You have also mistreated my sister," Efren replied.

"She was suspected of treason," he said, defending himself.

"I'm sure she has a few things to say on the subject," Efren stated.

The doors opened, allowing the princess inside. She had been listening to the conversation and was angry that Tyrol still believed her a traitor. "It isn't true!" she cried, rushing to King Tyrol's side. "I did nothing against the Kingdom of Na'zora." Turning to face her brother, a lump rose to her throat. "My crimes are against Ra'jhou. I wish only to be reunited with my son."

Tyrol thought for a moment. "My grandson is heir to the throne now that my son is gone. Rayne cannot leave, but I will grant you permission to return and live with him. You shall be treated as a princess and a widow."

"Is that acceptable to you, Aubriana?" Efren asked.

"It is," she replied, tears filling her eyes.

"I expect her to be treated well," Efren said. "Any rumor of her mistreatment will be met with military action."

King Tyrol nodded. "You have my word."

"Then our two kingdoms shall know peace," Efren declared. "I have no desire to continue this war." After a pause, he added, "You shall stay as my guest until my wife returns."

Once again, Tyrol was escorted by dwarves. This time they walked next to him rather than dragging him. Their firm grips still held tight to his arms, in case the king decided to take a different route than the one they had planned. Leading him to the lowest level of the castle, they showed him to a room with no windows and only a straw bed for furniture.

"This is your room," one of the dwarves grunted. "Enjoy your stay."

Slamming the door behind them, the dwarves left the king in silence. He was fuming with anger, his teeth clenched tightly. What right did they have to keep him prisoner? He had agreed to all of Ra'jhou's terms.

Lieutenant Jak appeared outside the door. With a knock, he said, "Majesty what are your orders?"

"See that their wretched queen is returned here at once!" he shouted through the door. "And get me out of here!"

Chapter 43

Aubriana made ready to depart immediately.

Though she loved the land of Ra'jhou dearly, she would gladly live in Na'zora next to her son, the heir to the kingdom's throne. With his mother to watch over him, he would learn to become a proper king. She would make sure King Tyrol did not have any influence over him. No longer would she be the weak, eager-to-please princess she had been before. From now on, she would be strong, like Ryshel. She would speak out and take a stand when necessary, and she would not let others determine what was best for her own son. If she had to fight for him, she would. Ra'jhou had proved itself a powerful kingdom, and she hoped she and her son would be welcome to return here should life in Na'zora prove too difficult.

Shala prepared the princess's luggage and saw that it was loaded into a carriage. A second carriage waited in the courtyard to carry the two ladies to the palace. As she made her way down the stairs, Aubriana realized there was one more thing she needed to do before departing.

It was still early, and Efren had not yet arrived at his throne room. Hurrying down the corridor, she hoped to catch him before he was surrounded by nobles and servants. What she needed to say was a private matter between brother and sister.

Arriving outside his bedchamber, she hesitated a moment before knocking. To her surprise, Efren himself opened the door. He was dressed rather plainly, considering his day would be spent at court discussing the rebuilding of his kingdom.

"Good morning, dear brother," she said. "I'm set to leave for Na'zora, and I wanted to say goodbye."

Efren reached out for her hand and squeezed it. "I wish you well, my sister," he said. "Give Rayne my love."

Nervously, she asked, "Can you ever forgive me? My mistake has cost you much, and I deeply regret my actions. I cannot express—"

"Think of it no more," he said, interrupting her. "The matter is done."

Aubriana nodded, wiping the tears from her eyes. "I love you, Efren," she said. "You are the finest king this land has ever known. I hope you will allow me to visit on occasion."

Efren held his sister tightly to his chest. "I love you too," he replied. "You are always welcome here, and I look forward to our next meeting. Now go. Your son is waiting."

* * * * *

Footsteps hurried toward Ryshel's cell as she sat in the darkness. Rising to her feet, she saw the face of the young guard as he approached. Rattling his keys, he unlocked the door and opened it wide.

"What's going on?" she asked, her voice cracking. She feared this might be the day of her execution.

"I am to escort you to the palace." Hesitating a moment, he added, "My lady."

"Am I to be put on trial?" she wondered aloud.

"No, Your Majesty," he responded. "You are to be treated as an honored guest."

Ryshel could hardly believe her ears. What had occurred to warrant such a drastic change? "Please," she said. "Tell me what has happened."

Leading her away from the prison, the guard said, "A messenger arrived this morning with word from the king. You are to be released and taken back to Ra'jhou immediately."

"But how did the king know I was here?"

The guard paused in his walking and turned to face the queen. "Our army was defeated, and Ra'jhou's king, your husband, has threatened to invade Na'zora if you are not released unharmed." He stared at her a moment, still shocked to discover she was truly a queen as she had insisted.

Ryshel was led inside the palace to an expansive chamber. Four ladies had been assigned to tend to her needs, and they greeted her as she stepped inside the room. A warm bath was prepared for her, and she gladly removed her clothing and sank into the tub.

"You might as well burn that dress," she said to one servant. "You'll never wash away the smell of that prison." She rubbed her skin vigorously, hoping the same was not true for herself. "Bring more rosewater," she commanded them. Never before had she been a demanding person, but today was different. Her kingdom now had the upper hand, though she did not know how.

As she relaxed in the warm water, a smile spread over her face. How had Efren managed to defeat the Na'zorans? He was a clever man, but what he had accomplished was nearly impossible. *It's too bad he didn't send a personal message for me,* she thought. She looked forward to hearing the rest of the story.

After soaking for more than an hour, Ryshel finally rose from her bath. She was given a fine golden gown that had belonged to the previous queen of Na'zora. With her servants trailing behind her, she made her way through the palace to visit with Rayne.

"Auntie Rysh!" he cried upon seeing her. He ran to greet her, wrapping his arms around her waist.

"How are you, sweet child?" she asked, looking at his shining face. A twinge of pain entered her heart as she thought of her own children. Hopefully, they had been spared knowledge of her imprisonment. The last thing she wanted was for them to worry about her. She longed to reunite with them.

"I'm taking the prince to Ra'jhou to his mother," she declared to her servants.

"My lady, the king has forbidden it!" one of them replied. "His mother is on her way here."

Ryshel was displeased by the news. It was best for Rayne to reside in Ra'jhou. "Are you certain of this?"

"Yes, my lady," the woman responded. "The princess has already departed and will be here any day now."

Ryshel wasn't sure why Aubriana would choose to reside in Na'zora, but there was nothing else she could do. She would have to wait until Aubriana arrived before she could depart. Leaving Rayne alone in the hands of the Na'zorans was not an option. Without his mother to protect him, he would need Ryshel as his advocate. Though it pained her to stay away from her own family, there was no other choice. Her stay in Na'zora was not yet over.

Chapter 44

Morning arrived and found Efren alone in his bedchamber once more. Each day without Ryshel was agony, even in what should be his moment of glory. His kingdom was safe, and his people were no longer in danger. Ryshel, on the other hand, was still in Na'zora, or somewhere in between the two kingdoms. He had heard no word from her, and he had no information as to her safety. Her absence weighed heavily on his heart, and he longed for her to return to him.

This morning he was preparing to address his people to let them know that he would not forget about them. There was an entire kingdom to be rebuilt, including several key cities. Farms had been destroyed, and trade had been halted to all major markets. All of these things would take time to repair, but as long as his people were willing to work hard, their goals would be accomplished. He looked forward to having his kingdom restored. It would shine once more, as it had in the days of peace he had enjoyed as a child.

A large crowd gathered in the castle courtyard to listen to the king's address. There had been plenty to celebrate since the defeat of the Na'zorans. No Ra'jhouan lives had been lost during the siege, thanks to the appearance of the dwarven army.

Arden escorted the king to the castle walls to speak to the crowd. It was a beautiful day without any clouds above to interrupt the blue of the sky. The sun's rays sent warmth to touch the faces of the gathered citizens. Eagerly they watched as the king took his place above them.

Stepping out into the sunlight, Efren drew in a deep breath. The air smelled of hope, and the birds chirped happily overhead, unaware of the destruction that had occurred in their kingdom. Standing proudly upon the wall, a broad smile spread across his face. "People of Ra'jhou," he said to the crowd.

Immediately, the citizens began to cheer and applaud. Their king had led them to victory and saved all their lives. The people were well aware that he had arranged the alliance between Ra'jhou and the dwarves, and they had been informed about his marvelous invention. They were proud to call him their king, and they celebrated the sight of him upon the wall.

"People of Ra'jhou," he repeated. Finally, the crowd quieted, allowing him to speak. "Our kingdom is safe!" The crowd cheered again, and he paused to allow them to finish before continuing his speech. "There is still much work to be done. Rebuilding will take time, and we must work together to ensure each of you has a home to go back to. We have lost much, but together, we shall rebuild and restore the beauty of Ra'jhou. I will personally travel to each district to be certain the work is going as planned."

The crowd erupted in applause. No king in their lifetime had bothered to visit each portion of the kingdom. The thought of having the king walk among them gave them a sense of pride, especially among the poorer citizens.

Turning to Arden, Efren said, "Invite the leaders of the dwarf army for a conference. I would like to speak with them."

"Of course, Your Majesty," Arden said, bowing.

The leaders of the dwarf army soon assembled within the throne room. Pedr stood proudly at the front, his face beaming as the king took his seat.

"Pedr," Efren began, "I cannot begin to express my gratitude to your people."

"Think nothing of it," the dwarf replied. "Your silver has placed me back in my own king's good graces. Though I admit I had to offer him a higher percentage of the profits than I wanted to."

"Do not trouble yourself with that," Efren responded. "No amount of silver could ever compare with the safety of my people. I am in your debt."

"I am the one who is indebted to you," Pedr stated. "Without your help, I would never have been allowed to set foot in my homeland again. Now I have a mine to run and trade between our kingdoms to oversee."

"Then we have both found victory," Efren replied. "There shall be free trade between our two peoples from now on. I would have your finest general train my men into a true fighting force. Ra'jhou has never had an army that would equal the strength of the dwarves. I would have us prepared for any future invasion."

"That's a wise plan," Pedr replied. "I have a few men in mind who would be honored to hold such a position. Groot and his apprentices have already begun crafting new weapons for your troops. Your men's weapons were inferior to that of your enemy, but they will never be so again."

"There is also the matter of your new settlement along my northern border," Efren said. "I invite you to settle within the borders of Ra'jhou. I know you have a camp at the outskirts, but that is not territory that I can claim. That area is occasionally visited by the Wild Elves who live among the forests. They may not take kindly to your people living there."

"I'd be honored to build a village within your borders," Pedr replied. "The area just outside the mine will do nicely, and my people will appreciate the added protection of being within your kingdom."

Efren stood to shake hands with the dwarf who had arranged Ra'jhou's military victory. He owed this man a great deal, and he would see to it that he was repaid in every way possible.

Pedr marched proudly from the throne room, ready for his journey north. It was time to reunite with his kinsmen and begin building the new life they had come here to find. There would be more challenges along the way, but Pedr looked forward to facing them. The home he had lost in the mountains would be replaced with one in Ra'jhou. With his own hands, he would see to the building of a community—one he could take pride in. Serving an honorable king would bring him honor of his own.

Chapter 45

"It won't be long now, my lady," Shala said in an effort to calm Aubriana's nerves. The princess had been restless since she entered the carriage, and the long ride was not helping the situation.

Aubriana nodded. "It seems to be getting farther away the longer we travel," she said. "It feels like we're never going to arrive."

"We're less than a day away now," Shala informed her.

"I hope he's being treated well," Aubriana said. "With the king away, there's no way to know if his orders are being carried out."

"Queen Ryshel is at his side," Shala reminded her. "Don't worry, my lady. He is safe. I'm sure of it."

Again Aubriana nodded. She wanted to believe Shala, but until she had her son in her arms, she could not be certain. Ryshel was supposed to be out of prison, but there had been no word at the time of Aubriana's departure. She hoped the queen was safe, and that she was being treated well at the hands of the Na'zorans.

"Shall we play a game, my lady?" Shala asked, trying to calm the princess. She produced a deck of cards from her bag and shuffled them.

Aubriana only pretended to care about the game. Her mind was whirling with possibilities, and it was too difficult to concentrate on the rules. After losing two hands, she bid Shala to put the cards away.

As the carriage continued to roll, Aubriana stared out her window, hoping to see familiar terrain that would indicate her arrival at the palace. Finally, after days of travel, the palace came into view. Aubriana could hardly contain her excitement. "We've arrived!" she shouted. "The palace is just ahead!"

Shala sighed, relieved to finally be back at the palace. Any longer and she was certain the princess would have clawed her way through the carriage walls.

Aubriana barely waited for the carriage to come to a stop before she flung open the door. Without the aid of any servants, she exited the carriage and ran up the palace steps. The marble floors echoed beneath her feet as she ran through the palace to her son's room. To her delight, he had not been moved. His laughter filled her ears, nearly stopping her heart. Pushing open the door to his chamber, she beheld Ryshel seated on the floor, with Rayne in her arms. She was reading him a story, and he was elated.

Looking up from the book, Ryshel smiled warmly at the princess. Pointing, she whispered to Rayne, "Look who's home."

The little boy looked up to see his mother, and immediately jumped to his feet. "Mommy!" he cried as he ran to her.

With tears rolling down her cheeks, Aubriana scooped her son into her arms and squeezed him tightly. Showering him with kisses, she said, "I love you so much." Rising to her feet, she also hugged Ryshel. "You have risked your life for my son, and I shall never forget it. Thank you, Sister." She kissed Ryshel on both cheeks.

"He's a sweet little boy," Ryshel said. "He has missed you greatly."

Hugging Rayne to her side, she said, "You must be missing your own children, but will you at least stay the night? We could have dinner together, and you could depart first thing in the morning."

Ryshel did not want to refuse Aubriana's offer, but she was aching to return to her home. "I've been away too long already," she said. "I was hoping to return immediately upon your arrival."

"I understand," Aubriana replied. "My journey here felt like an eternity." Reaching out to hug Ryshel one last time, she added, "Have a safe journey, Sister."

With a nod, Ryshel rushed to her room, which was situated next to Rayne's. Without the aid of servants, she packed the few possessions she had acquired into a small bag and exited the palace. Aubriana's coach had not yet departed. Her belongings were still being unloaded.

Approaching the coachman, Ryshel asked, "Can you take me back to Ra'jhou?"

"I can, Your Majesty," he replied. "But I'll need some time to get fresh horses."

"Of course," she said with a sigh. Any delay was painful, as she desired nothing more than to return home to her family. A carriage, however, was not the only means of transportation. Deciding on another course of action, she headed to the royal stables.

Hurrying to the rear of the palace, she paid no mind to the dirt that was collecting upon the tail of her dress. This was no time to bother with proper manners. Her heart desired home, and she did not care if she arrived a mess. Stepping inside the stables, she declared, "I desire a horse."

"These horses belong to the king, my lady," the stable hand replied, looking down at his shoes.

"The king has given his permission, I assure you. I am Queen Ryshel of Ra'jhou, and I need you to saddle a horse for me this instant."

"Right away, Your Majesty," the boy said, running to obey her command. Within minutes, he had a black horse saddled and ready to go.

"Do you have anything I can use for a bed along the trail?" she asked, knowing she would have to make camp at night since she would not be sleeping inside a carriage.

"I have a bedroll here," the boy said. "And a blanket too. They are stored for servant use and not fit for a queen." The boy spoke in a hushed tone, almost ashamed he had mentioned such poor items to a noble lady.

"Those will do nicely," she replied.

Without question, the boy retrieved the items and tied them behind the horse's saddle. He led the horse to the queen and offered her the reins.

Taking the reins, Ryshel hopped up onto the horse's back. Reaching into her purse, she drew out two gold coins and tossed them to the boy. "For your services," she said. Nudging the horse forward, she set out toward Ra'jhou.

Chapter 46

Racing across the landscape with the wind rippling through her hair, Ryshel felt truly free. It had been too long since she'd enjoyed the simple pleasure of going for a ride. She dreaded the thought of having to stop and make camp, but neither she nor the horse were capable of going forever. Her journey would take time, but she would push herself as far as she could before stopping.

As she crossed the border into Ra'jhou, she witnessed firsthand the devastation that had occurred in her kingdom. Villages stood in ruins, farmlands were burned, and there was no sign of life. Staring at the remains, she realized she had slowed the horse to a walk. Though she yearned to be home, she could not take her eyes off the senseless waste of life and land.

Dismounting, she entered the burned-out village for a closer look.

A charred doll caught her eye among the rubble. Kneeling down to pick it up, she turned the blackened toy over in her hand. Had the child survived? Would Na'zora's mages have spared her? Ryshel was certain they wouldn't. How better to instill fear into your prey than to murder children? A gentle rain began to fall, stirring the soot that remained. Ryshel coughed slightly, taking one last look at the village. Mounting her horse, she continued along her way, dreading what else she might see.

A full day passed before she came upon the next village. This time, she did not stop. Her heart was still heavy from the first, and this would only add to her sorrow. How could such loss ever be replaced? She knew many of her citizens were safe within the castle, but she wondered how many had been lost. Even one was too many.

For days she rode on, passing village after village. No place was left untouched by the war. Finally, the mountains came into view, and the castle was visible in the distance. Her mood turned lighter as she imagined her reunion with her children. Never again would she leave them, not even for a day.

As she approached the castle, trumpets rang out. A scout had spotted her and recognized her as the queen. Duke Arden took note of the commotion and made his way to the castle steps. Ryshel was dismounting her horse as he reached her.

"Daughter," he said, wrapping his arms around her. "It's good to see you."

She squeezed her father tightly. "I feel like I've been away forever," she said. "You must tell me everything. How did Efren manage this victory?"

"He arranged an alliance with the dwarves," he explained. "Not only that, he stopped all supplies to Na'zora's mages from the elves of the islands, and he invented a weapon that explodes on impact."

Ryshel stared open-mouthed at her father. "How did he manage these things? And how did he keep them secret?"

"After Aubriana's betrayal, he trusted no one fully. He's had servants switched out repeatedly, and told the rest of us only bits and pieces of his plans."

"He probably needed me," she said with regret. Her eyes looked to the ground. "I should have been here."

"Things here could not have gone better," Arden replied. "You did what you felt you should do, and Rayne is safe and sound because of it." He hugged his daughter once more before ascending the steps at her side. "Let's let the king know you've returned," he said with a smile.

The sound of the trumpets had already alerted the king. A servant had announced the queen's arrival and had summoned the royal children. They stood together with their father in the corridor, awaiting Ryshel's entrance.

Upon seeing her children, Ryshel dropped to her knees and spread her arms wide. Hugging all three of them together, she could not contain her tears. "I've missed you so much," she declared. Kissing each of them, she repeated "I love you" to each one.

Rising to her feet, she stepped forward to her husband, who stood patiently waiting for her to finish kissing the children. Without a word, Ryshel wrapped her arms around his neck, standing on tiptoe to squeeze him as tightly as possible. He buried his face in the crook of her neck as tears filled his eyes.

As they finished their embrace, Efren said, "I am incomplete without you, my love." Kissing her softly, he felt whole once more. Her familiar touch and the warmth of her presence had been sorely missed.

Taking his hand in hers, she promised, "I will never leave again without you at my side." This was a promise she intended to keep. From now on, they would act as a single unit, rather than two individuals.

"I guess we can send King Tyrol home now," Arden said, chuckling.

"He's still here?" Ryshel asked.

"Indeed," Efren replied. "He has been a guest in our cellars, awaiting your safe arrival."

"Is it safe to release him?" she wondered. "He might return with an army."

"That's unlikely," Efren responded. "The dwarf army is still here, and they've agreed to stay during the rebuilding. He will have to wait until he's sure they're gone before he tries anything. I don't think he'll be too eager to face those firebombs again. He has no mages left and little chance of gaining more."

"I've seen the devastation he caused our kingdom," she said, looking down. "He does not deserve to go free. He should answer for his crimes."

"Punishing him further may result in a renewal of hostilities with Na'zora," Arden cautioned. "Rayne is far too young to ascend the throne, and rivals might come forward should King Tyrol meet his demise."

"I agree," Efren replied. "We must send him home unharmed. For now, only his pride is wounded.

Causing strife within his kingdom might prove detrimental to our own."

"Then let him go," she said. "Perhaps he will bring punishment upon himself someday."

"Our dwarf friends are helping strengthen our army," Efren informed her. "We will not be so weak if Tyrol chooses to invade again in the future."

Ryshel nodded, trusting in her husband's wisdom. He had already proved himself a competent wartime leader. Gathering her children to her side, she asked, "Shall we sit in the gardens? I long to look upon the mountains awhile."

Together they stepped out into the sunlight, making their way to the gardens. The gardens were green and pleasant, as if no war had visited the kingdom. The battle had ceased before they were destroyed, as the villages on the outskirts had been. In time, Ryshel knew the entire kingdom would be restored to this same level of beauty. Soon the people would have new homes and farms, and once again the kingdom would prosper. All they needed was time and the leadership of a devoted king.

Taking his wife in his arms, Efren said, "It's good to have you back." He kissed her soft lips and hugged her tightly. His family was once again complete, and his kingdom had not been lost. Despite his reluctance to take the throne, he had proved himself a capable and loving ruler. He took joy in the presence of his reunited family. With Ryshel at his side, he would rule over many long years of peace.

About the Author

Lana Axe lives in the Missouri countryside surrounded by dogs, cats, birds, and reptiles. She spends most of her free time daydreaming about elves, magic, and far-away lands.

For more information, please visit: lana-axe.com.